Solitary

Jenny Leidecker

The characters and events portrayed in this book are fictitious. Any similarity to real persons, living or dead, is coincidental and not intended by the author.

No part of this book may be reproduced, or stored in a retrieval system, or transmitted in any form or by any means, electronic, mechanical, photocopying, recording, or otherwise without express written permission of the publisher.

ISBN-13: 979-8-9868726-2-9

Printed in the United States of America

Also by Jenny Leidecker

Into the Dark
Shhh
Invisible
Lucky
Caged

www.jennyleidecker.com

Jenny Leidecker

SHHH...

ONE

People have told me to be quiet, to shut up, and to shhh a lot in my life. I don't think this has everything to do with the fact that I'm a girl, contrary to some arguments. There is some truth in that position, and there have been many a time when myS double X chromosome has been the deciding factor in someone thinking they had the right to stifle my words. However, my inability to close my mouth and stop talking about whatever it is I happen to be passionate about at that moment, that has been the catalyst more times than I can count. The only note on every single report card growing up I ever received was, "Jenny is a very bright girl, but she sure does talk a lot." Well, I guess maybe, I've just always had a lot to say. Isn't that possible?

The problem is that I'll chatter to the point of obsession, and it can be more than some people know how to handle. Lord help those in the vicinity if I find a fellow professional talker; that is a situation that could go on for hours and up to the point of near starvation. I'm not sure I can help myself if I'm honest, and I have a gift of circling the conversation back around gracefully to the topic of my interest. Before you know it, we're back discussing Mozart, my current writing project, or even my cat after you somehow managed to try and direct us to current foreign policy issues.

There's a laundry list of subjects I can fall into at any given moment, and to be clear, not one of them is laundry. Although, to be fair, I have had a few drawn-out discussions regarding the need for your own sheet washing day[1] and the art of folding a fitted sheet correctly. Yes, I am one of those people who sold part of their soul to the devil in order to be able to produce a flattened square out of a cinched clunky bottom sheet, and it was worth it. And to fully assess my level of laundry craziness, I will fold my sheets directly out of the dryer, walk the thirty or so steps to my bed, just to unfold them and make it. Let's not even try to determine the number of randomly ridiculous things I do week in and week out. I don't have that kind of time.

I should say that I'm also an excellent listener, and my sometimes constant (try and reconcile that thought in your brain) inability to keep the subject matter to the topic you'd like to discuss isn't my disinterest. It's just I have finally lost the battle to the monkeys jumping around for attention in my head, that's all. They're loud and disruptive and make it nearly impossible to concentrate on anything

---

1 - I highly recommend having your very own sheet washing day every week. I suggest Fridays, as this will allow you to curl up Friday night and sleep comfortable late into your Saturday morning on those wonderfully clean and crisp sheets. The smell of dreams holding onto you tightly. It truly is an amazing feeling.

else. If you watch closely as I wildly discuss the latest novel I just read that had this fantastic scene[2], here, let me tell it to you; you'll see one of those monkeys escape and run off in a different direction. You'd think that would stop me, but the next one is standing there waiting, somehow managing to string together a conversation about strange ancient rituals into how to bake bread using applesauce, and somehow ending up with a story about how my cat has learned to turn off the light switch and likes to do so as a joke while I try to write. I don't find it funny, but he's pursuing a career in stand up and who am I to squash anyone else's dream?

I guess what I'm getting at here is that I have more experience than most with that Shhhhh-ing sound, I mean, unless you're a librarian, but boy have they had to use those skills in my presence on numerous occasions. Pretty sure I have kept some of their shhhh-ing fingers in tip-top shape over the last forty years, much to their chagrin. I can remember how shocking it was the first few times it happened. Teachers telling me to stop mid-thought, my parents were trying to convince me to stop long enough to take a breath, and even my peers, tired of hearing me have an opinion on every single topic they brought up or some strange fact to go along with it that I had found in a book I read the other day. For as much as I might be a professional talker, I have incited some professional grade shhhh-ing in return.

It never deterred me, though, which either proves that I'm stubborn as hell or terrible at picking up on certain social cues. In truth, I'm likely suffering from a bit of both. Here's my school of thought on

---

2 - This is a constant in most conversations I have. Feel free to reach out. Let's discuss our current reads.

the subject, we're always learning, always growing, and as we fill ourselves with new knowledge and information and find these new passions, some of it can't help but spill over and out of our ears or in my case, out of my mouth. Those monkeys start eating the furniture in the waiting room, and there hasn't been a magazine up there that was in any form of reading condition for years. This is where the real story begins, my monkeys multiplying like gremlins that had jumped into an Olympic-sized pool right after pulling through the drive-thru at one in the morning, thinking this all sounded like a good plan after a night filled with heavy drinking. Let's just say there were more monkeys than I could handle anymore, and I could feel the pressure of their needed release trying to make my head explode. I needed to show some of them the door before they took over and ate away my ability to function in normal society. At least as normal as I had been able to be up to this point anyway.

SHHH...

TWO

I woke up that morning with the worst headache I can ever remember having in my life. Splitting or pounding didn't come close to what I was experiencing. It felt more like all of those monkeys had taken up hammers and were bashing into my gray matter in unison. My worst hangover or migraine couldn't compare to what I was feeling. I looked over at the cat as if he had something to do with it.

"Did you spend last night pouncing on my head, and I just didn't know it? Or have you been dousing my water with headache pills?"

His eyes flew open wide when I started to talk, and with a hiss and an arch of his back, he jumped into the air and flew away down the hallway. Not sure what managed to get into him all of a sudden but see if I rush to pull the lid on your can today. The pain subsided just long enough for me to notice, and then it was back, with just as many hammers as before, pounding away. Reaching into the medicine cabinet, I poured out a couple of ibuprofen. I swallowed them instantly, hoping they'd work fast because I was pretty sure the cat hissing at me wasn't going to cure anything. In fact, it would likely lead to him running through the kitchen to knock over his water bowl for laughs. Another one of his stand up acts he had nearly perfected. He always managed to make everyone else bust a gut watching him slide into his water like a bowling ball of a kitten attempting to knock down all of the invisible pins. I did not find it as funny, but maybe the part about being the human stuck cleaning it up was where the humor of it lost me.

None of that mattered now, I could barely think straight from the pain, and I wasn't quite sure how I would maneuver my way through everything I needed to get done. No matter what I tried, it wouldn't subside. Showering and grabbing a cup of coffee, I was hoping that by the time I made it to the car, I'd be able to focus enough to drive on to my first destination. With all the errands I needed to run today, I couldn't afford to stay laid up in bed with this headache. Gathering up my bag, I almost made it to the door when my phone rang. Dropping everything with a groan, I reached into my back pocket and recognized a long conversation in the making. I wasn't about to drive and talk on the phone and deal with this headache all at once. The muscles around my head were throbbing to the rhythm of the monkey chain gang working nonstop on what had to be the transcontinental railroad or something. I fell back onto the couch. I might as well be comfortable for this one and slid my thumb across the screen to answer the vibrating monster in my hand.

"Hey, Mom."

The sigh of irritation reaching the hundreds of

miles to the other end of the call, and there was no way she didn't hear it.

"Hey, Sweetie. You alright? It can't be that bad already; you couldn't have been out of bed for too long."

That's right. Obviously, I'm a lazy, incompetent woman who sleeps all day and does nothing but watch reruns and the home shopping channels all night. With a roll of my eyes, I groaned, both actions just increasing the pain. I swear it felt like my skull was starting to crack from the pressure, and for a second, I contemplated a trip to the emergency room as my first stop on my journey of tasks to fulfill today.

"Yeah, I'm fine, just woke up with the worst headache."

"Did you take anything for it?"

Of course not. I'm an idiot that hasn't learned about the healing powers of ibuprofen. Surely, I've decided that burning some sage or standing on my head was the only proper way to heal this infliction. Probably should have tried both of those before reaching into the medicine cabinet, then I wouldn't be complaining about it still. I rolled my eyes again at the thought, having not learned my lesson the first time, and winced in response.

"Yes, of course, I took some medicine for it, and I wish it would hurry up and kick in already."

"Well, you don't have to snap at me about it. I was just asking. I am your mother, you know. I do actually care, regardless of why you think I'm asking."

Oh great, let's toss in a little guilt for good measure. I mean, what good is the pain if there isn't some proper suffering added on top of it? Come to think of it, most of my conversations with her end with a headache. They don't usually start with one. Heaven help me if she adds to this thing; my head will truly explode for sure. Taking a deep breath in an attempt to settle my voice so as not to poke the passive-aggressive bear caged on the other end of this call, I added just enough calm and sweetness before responding. It's a delicate balance. Too much and she'll accuse me of being condescending, but too little, and this whole conversation is going to spiral into an argument over how little I understand how much she cares and what all she has sacrificed as a mother and blah, blah, blah. Luckily, it's a skill I have mastered over the years, just not sure it's one I have as much control over in my current state.

"Yes, I know, Mom. Honestly, I'm just in a lot of pain, and I have too much to do to sit here and deal with this headache on top of it. I probably should eat a little something too now that I think about it."

Tossing in the possibility of being hangry helps to cover a multitude of sins when it comes to tone, and if that isn't enough, I'll casually throw out how I'm about to start my period for good measure. Whatever I have to do not to end up on the guilt train this conversation could easily buy a first-class ticket to in an instant, I'm willing to make that sacrifice today. No matter what I do, this conversation will not allow any medicine I've taken to do its job, and the two will end up likely evening each other out.

"You haven't eaten yet? Don't you know what time it is? You can't honestly be leaving to run errands without something in your stomach. Are you trying to pass out in public from low blood sugar? I swear, it's like you don't even think sometimes."

Dammit! This is what a headache will get me. I

should have realized that it could have gone either way. Always start with the period excuse, always. Taking a deep breath and getting up to grab a granola bar so she can hear me chewing away over here, I head back to the bathroom for another round of ibuprofen. Whatever was causing the headache in the first place, it was no match for my mother's ability to create a migraine in less than an hour from the other side of the planet, much less a twenty-minute phone conversation with lecturing on her to-do list this morning. She was on a roll, and nothing was going to deter her need to tell someone what they should be doing today. Unfortunately, that appeared to be my role this morning. How I long for the days when she isn't talking to me first, and my brother is at the top of her list to call instead of me. I don't need to look at any horoscope to know that luck is not on my side today, and I wasn't about to get a word in, or at least not many this morning. I might as well cook a full breakfast instead, I have plenty of time, and I wince again at the uncontrollable eye roll. I need to learn how to get a handle on those one of these days, and with another sigh, I head into the kitchen.

SHHH...

THREE

By the time she had finished running down the list of everything I had been doing wrong in my life, I had taken more medicine, had a second cup of coffee and a full breakfast, complete with bacon. However, the headache remained and was hurting so badly that I'm not sure if it was any better or, for that matter, any worse. I walked into the bathroom one last time to check the recommended dosage on the bottle, only to realize I had reached the maximum for at least the next six hours. Groaning, I tossed the bottle back into place and only barely caught myself from slamming the cabinet shut. No need to add any self-inflicted pain to today, and I closed it quieter than I thought was humanly possible instead.

Catching my reflection in the mirror one last time before trying to leave, I noticed something on my lip. Is that blood? Am I bleeding? I hadn't had a nosebleed since being "accidentally" knocked in the nose with my brother's elbow when I was thirteen. I still don't believe he didn't do it on purpose. If I hadn't just told him to suck it up after getting in trouble with mom because he had failed his math test and was hiding it in his backpack that I may have told her about, maybe I would have believed it was an accident. As it were, he timed it well, no witnesses but me and my nose, and well, he was my mother's baby. Bloody nose or not, I was the one yelled at for getting in the way of his elbow.

"Honestly, Jenny, you really should be more careful and pay closer attention to your surroundings."

That was the motherly love I received that afternoon. Well, that and the whole, "don't get any of that on my carpet," tossed over her shoulder as she walked out of the room to do something much more important than deal with my bloody nose. Don't get me wrong; she's not a bad mother by any means. She's just not a great mother by any stretch of the imagination either. None of that matters right this minute. What matters is this stream of blood pouring from my left nostril. How do you stop a bloody nose anyway? I've never had to deal with this. Do I pinch it and lean my head back? I remember someone mentioning ice or something like that at one point in my forty years of gathering useless information that is in no way helping me as I stand here frozen staring in the mirror. So, I do what any grown person in my shoes would do, wad up a little toilet paper, and lean around the corner asking the great know-it-all that is my smarter than me home device.

"How do you stop a bloody nose?"

As soon as she responds with, "According to WebMD," I'm rounding the corner yelling for it to stop. The last thing I need today is for some electronic chick to tell me I'm dying because of a simple nosebleed. I feel as if I'm halfway there already as it is; no sense adding fuel to that anxiety fire. Grabbing my phone out of my back pocket, I dial up my best friend. She's injured herself enough to qualify as an entire football team, and she'll have an answer on what to do.

"Wow, you're up early, everything ok? Did someone die?"

Great, maybe I am a little lazier than I realize. Still, I don't have it in me to argue my less than sloth-like capabilities, and just because she gets up at the ass crack of dawn every day doesn't mean that my wake up time is any less conducive to productivity than hers is. Not every day anyway. Rolling my eyes for the hundredth or so time this morning, I groaned at the pain that was relentless and had yet to subside even a little.

"No one died, but I feel like this headache might kill me. Oh, and thanks for that welcoming good morning, I get up early sometimes."

She broke in laughing at my comment, and I had to admit, I was trying to convince myself way more than I was ever going to be able to get her to believe such a statement. This morning was not going anywhere near how I had planned it to, and my irritation quota is reaching its limit fast.

"Yeah, sure you do. You have an appointment this morning, or did that cat of yours turn into an unwanted alarm clock again?"

I could have handled him running full tilt at my head with claws out at six in the morning more than all the other crap I have to filter through today, that's for damn sure. At least I would have forgotten about that by now and might have only been reminded of it from the pain of washing my hair. In fact, if I could just get this headache to go away, I'll never complain about blood loss from cat claws again, no matter how deep the cut may go. I promise. Nope, that's a lie. There is no way the shock of being Ginsu-ed out of the blue by the fluffy, sometimes loving, and cuddling roommate isn't going to elicit some choice words, sideways glances, and an ancient curse or two. If I'm going to try and start to bargain the pain away, I should start with something more believable.

"No, he's innocent, this morning at least. Although he's been dragging around this new toy lately, it's this stuffed doll with floppy legs. I swear it's almost as long as he is. You should see it. He parades around like he's killed it and should be praised by the villagers or something. Come to think about it, not sure what that might say about our relationship. Hmmm. Anyway, I called for a real reason. How the hell do you stop a nosebleed?"

"Do you have a nosebleed? Jesus, Jenny, what did you do?"

Why is it always my fault? Why couldn't it just be some random medical issue entirely out of the blue that I'm dealing with and not that I walked into a door? Just because she's seen me walk into a door doesn't mean that's what happened this time. I'm not that clumsy, am I? The number of bruises and broken toes stand up in unison with the affirmative, and this morning just keeps getting better. All I need now is for someone to remind me that I haven't finished the half dozen projects I've been working on for too long, and my day will be complete. Better than a theme park, that's my life today. Jeez, I just need to crawl back into bed and declare today over and done with already, and if it weren't for the fact that after cooking my breakfast, there is nothing in my kitchen but an Old Mother Hubbard situation, I would.

Pulling the wad of toilet paper out from under my nose, the paper is red, but my nose is no longer dripping. Thank god, who knew those things could just stop? Learn something new every day, I guess.

"I didn't do anything, thank you very much. And my nose was bleeding, but it's stopped now, so your expert-level knowledge is no longer necessary. You know, I haven't had one of those since I was a kid. Not sure what brought it on, and if I didn't know any better, I'd blame it on this headache of mine. I can't get the damn thing to go away. Granted, my mother called just as I was getting ready to walk out the door, and that was almost an hour of her telling me all the things I've been doing wrong, and all the wonderful things my brother's been up to here lately. Of course, she had to update me on the entire neighborhood as well. Oh yeah, local telenovela airing of dirty laundry, her neighbors have gone from just arguing loud enough for her to hear from the backyard, I swear she only planted that garden back there so she could listen in, but now the wife follows him to his car every morning yelling about some secretary. I'm guessing that one's going to end well, but I think we called that about a month or so ago when the big argument they had been having was over shutting the refrigerator door all the way, wasn't it?"

I almost didn't want to stop long enough for her to answer. It seemed the more I talked to her, the less my head hurt. I'm sure it's just the medicine finally kicking in, but man, I'm not sure I want to take any chances. This is the first bit of relief I've felt all day. It wasn't much, but enough to notice, and

I couldn't help but smile for the first time, thinking I might get over this affliction before lunch.

"Yeah, I think you're right. That one has been going on for a while. Did you say you're ok now? There must be something going around. I'm starting to get my own headache. If you're good, I'm going to go and grab some medicine and hopefully catch this before it gets out of hand. We better not be getting sick from you dragging us out to that bar the other night. I won't let you forget it if we are, I promise. I have that big presentation at work next week, and if I'm out because of some germ-infested hole in the wall you just had to go to, I'm going to kill you."

She didn't really mean kill me, but pretty damn close to it, I'm sure. She'd been trying to earn a promotion this entire year, and I knew if she aced this presentation, she was likely a shoo-in for it. God, I hope it wasn't that bar too. I had only heard about it from some guy I bumped into at the record store that they had this fantastic craft beer that I just had to try and well, had to is had to, isn't it? The man was buying a Sonny Rollins album, and anyone who can appreciate one of the greatest jazz saxophonists of all time, surely, they have great taste in beer too. He did not. Not only was the bar a dump, but the beer was watered down and tasted like something cheap. I would have happily drunk too much of out of a keg at some hidden party in high school. Lesson learned, great taste in music does not necessarily equate to equal footing in all other matters. That's a shame too. I would have used that as a litmus test for the rest of my life. I will never live this down if it's all my fault, and I could never forgive myself if it hurt her chances for that promotion she's been biting at the bit for and has earned a hundred times over already. Crossing my fingers and tossing up a prayer into the universe, I hoped my next statement was true.

"I'm sure it's just allergies. Probably why I ended up with a bloody nose in the first place; you'll be fine, it's just a headache, and it's not like you can catch it from me over the phone. Go grab some meds, and I'll talk to you later.'

I could hear her wince through the phone. Please, oh, please don't let this be my fault, and I groaned at the thought.

"You better be right. I've gotta go. Talk to you later, and if you get another nosebleed, lean forward and pinch it, and if you have an ice pack handy, use that. Gotta go."

"Let's hope I don't need your advice and that your headache goes away quicker than mine has."

I heard her groan at my words and mutter a 'yeah' or 'it better' into the phone and was gone. The world didn't feel like it was going to end as soon as I felt like it might before, and the pain had subsided just enough for me to feel confident that I can get some things checked off my list here after all. I needed to drop off a few bills, get groceries, and I was hoping my hairdresser ended up with a cancellation today, but that would be a bonus if she did. I also had to drop off some overdue library books and return a pair of jeans that didn't look as good on me at home as they did in the store's dressing room. I think some of those shops have funhouse mirrors installed to make their clothes look better on than they really do. I mean, why else would you pay over a hundred dollars for a pair of jeans unless your butt looked so good you've decided you should be buried in them with your ass in the air for everyone to appreciate it. Needless to say, I had things to do, and I had been burning daylight for too long and needed to get going, but first on the list, more coffee.

SHHH...

FOUR

Climbing into the car, I could feel the headache already returning. It was as if the more I just sat there, the worse it got. I knew another cup of coffee was not going to help the situation but sitting and people watching for a few minutes is always a fun idea. My favorite caffeine creators are just around the corner, and the added boost of sugar couldn't hurt my need for some energy to get started on this list. I was already going to feel more productive before I ordered my bastardized version of what can honestly no longer truly be actual coffee, but I would be able to mark through one thing on the list first. The library was on the way, and swinging through the parking lot, I pulled up to the night drop, and as each book hit with a thud in the metal box, I could feel the hammers start to swing harder. I sure do hope those monkeys like sugar because I was open to any negotiations at this point. What wouldn't I do for some relief?

I probably should have just pulled through and

not taken the extra time to park and walk in to order my coffee, but the dim lighting and comfy chairs were crying out, and was I really in that big of a hurry? I was. I had to get things done today, and I didn't want to carry anything over into tomorrow. I needed to get back to my regular schedule, which, according to everyone else, included a certain level of expected laziness. Still, with enough incentive and motivation, I could get shit done. I admit it was sometimes more than a little laziness, but it's the weekend for criminy's sake, and Monday is just around the corner already. Spending one day in bed flipping through channels or reading while inhaling chocolate chip cookies is an acceptable way to enjoy a Sunday now and then or every Sunday, whatever floats your boat, and well, mine is happily docked in the Do-Nothing Marina just about every weekend. I refuse to feel bad about it, so don't even try.

Walking in, the smell of freshly ground beans made me smile, and I couldn't wait to have my hands around my very own whipped cream covered coffee-flavored creamer, because let's be honest, one shot of espresso along with sixteen ounces of frothy milk, and is it really still a coffee? I grabbed my order covered in caramel and chocolate shavings and headed to the darkest and coziest corner in the room. It was my favorite spot. There was a comfy armchair big enough for me to curl up in if I wanted and a matching one across from it for when I brought friends here to sit and take up space with me for way longer than we should. I liked it for the quiet, for the seclusion. No one knew you were back here unless they happened upon you looking for their own soft place to land, which was rare. It was my spot.

Sucking in the first sip of caffeinated goodness, the

pain intensified. You don't realize how many facial muscles it requires to suck sugar through a straw until every single one of them hurt and are pounding in unison. I would have to suck it up, though, no pun intended, because there was no other option since that medicine has decided not to work in the least. Rubbing at my temples with one hand and holding the cold cup against the other side of my head, I try to relax and convince myself that the headache isn't as bad as it is, but deep down, it feels like my entire face is going to pop off and my head explode. I really should go to the emergency room or something. I have never felt more like a headache was going to actually kill me in my life. I'm sure it's a symptom of a hundred different ailments, but you're not about to catch me reading about an aneurysm over here in the corner. I'm not about to take any chances of creating some self-fulfilling prophecy in the back corner of an overpriced coffee bar. I would either have to live with it or pull up my bootstraps and admit I need to see a professional about it.

Opening my eyes, I catch just the tips of someone's shoes and looking up. I'm not too shocked to find the rest of the person attached to those toes. An older woman stood there with a smile wrapped around her face. She obviously was not in the same pain I was from the looks of it. She was hoping to sit in the chair across from me, and she was going to be the sweetest granny in the world. I just knew it, so there was no way I could say no to her. I could sense my own kind. She was going to be one of those professional talkers too, and this relaxing trip to get coffee and people watch was about to turn into a torturous talkfest. I wasn't going to be able to stop myself from participating either, no matter how bad the pain might be, but I wasn't sure it was going to be a cure for what ails me, likely more stoking the flames of the painful fire raging in my head. Those monkeys were still working double time, and I guess if I could kick a few of them out, it might not be too bad after all.

"Do you mind if I sit here, Sweetie?"

Yep, just as predicted, saccharine. My teeth were going to hurt from all the sweetness pouring from this woman before this was over with; I just knew it.

"No, of course not. Go ahead. I can't say that I'll be great company. My head is pounding so hard. I think John Henry might have been mistaking my head for a piece of steel today."

Groaning and rubbing my temple for good measure, I was hoping she'd catch the hint and move onto another random person sitting alone to chat with, but no such luck. She plopped down and settled into her natural role immediately.

"I hate to hear that. Can I offer you some pain relief? I'm pretty sure I have some aspirin in my bag here somewhere."

Smiling at her for the offer, I know she was trying to help, and it was nice for someone to just offer instead of assuming I didn't know how to take care of myself. Where was she this morning instead of my mother?

"No but thank you. I've already reached my designated limit for the moment, and I'm in a countdown with the clock while he sits and holds my next dosage hostage."

She laughed at my comment, not some, 'oh that was cute' kind of laugh, but she genuinely chuckled. Adjusting in my seat, I pulled up one leg and made myself comfortable. I already liked her, not because she laughed at my joke, although that did help, but because I could tell she was honest. Pain or not, I was going to enjoy meeting her today, and I'm sure she'll be able to part with some age-old wisdom that I didn't know when I sat down in here.

"No worries, it's nice to meet you. I'm Kay, it's really Katherine, but everyone has always called me Kay for as long as I can remember, which was too many years ago. I've practically lost count of them all."

"Hi Kay, I'm Jenny. I'd dare say you don't look a day of sixty, so I can't believe there's been that many years."

Smiling back at her and giggling at the comment. We both knew she was either knocking on eighty or recently passed it, but it wasn't a lie, she did look good for her age, and I meant what I said. She giggled back and swatted her hand in my direction. She knew I was flattering her, and well, when you live as long as she has, you deserve a bit of flattery here and there.

"Oh Sweetie, that's nice of you, but I've seen a few more decades than that, Dear. More than I probably should have had, and at this point, you're just excited you can roll out of bed and remember how to get dressed. I've been around long enough to know there's not a lot left for me to see. Probably why I tend to chat up strangers in coffee shops, living each minute the best I can. It's all I have left."

Never thought of it that way, and truth be told, I'll likely be Kay in another forty years, talking to anyone who'll acknowledge me. Today I could take long enough to listen. Even if it meant I didn't get everything done, it was going to be worth it. I just knew it. Headache be damned, I'm a professional, remember?

SHHH...

FIVE

"That's very sweet of you."

In all honesty, I had had a bit too much coffee myself, and I was listening to my mouth run at ninety miles an hour over there in my chair, and I needed to take a breath every once in a while. Walking back with the waters, I handed one to Kay and sat down again, ready to jump right back into conversation. Well, not really a conversation. She wasn't talking anymore, this was me telling, and she was the one on the listening end of things.

"There must be something in the air today. Mine seems to finally be settling down a bit, and my best friend was feeling it earlier when I was talking to her too."

The idea that my headache was contagious landed a thought for half a second, and I laughed at the prospect. I couldn't imagine giving someone else this pain, and honestly, it felt as if I was on the edge of my head exploding a few times today. Laughing again, titles like "Drama Queen" and "Cry

Baby" float by because there is no way a stinking headache was ever going to end me. That being said, I make a mental note to contact my doctor on Monday and make an appointment. I have no intention of going through this day again like it's on some never-ending loop without proper medication at my disposal. Shaking off the ridiculousness, I look back over at Kay, and she is starting to look as bad as I felt when I sat down here earlier.

"Are you sure you're ok?"

Nodding her head in response, she waves me on again. I'm not about to question her any further, and to be fair, there are monkeys waiting at that door that have been working hard all day slinging those sledgehammers, and I'm ready for them to get out. No vacancy. You don't have to go home, but you can't stay here anymore at the Brain Bar this morning, and before I knew it, my mouth and mind were off and running again.

"You know, talking about caffeine, one of my favorite songs is Cigarettes and Coffee."

That was all the lead in I needed to launch headfirst into a lecture of the best soul singers and songwriters. How there couldn't have been anyway, he knew that one of his songs would be so well known and loved that well over two hundred other artists have taken the time to record it. How intergenerational his sounds were and how they've lived on and will continue to for decades still. She smiled back at me, but I could tell it was pained. I asked her again.

"Are you sure you're not ready to head home or something? You don't look like you're feeling well."

"I'm fine. I'm fine. That aspirin ought to start kicking in here soon enough, but boy oh boy, do I feel like my head is ready to explode."

Her words hit home, and I knew exactly how she felt. I couldn't have described it any other way myself if you had asked me just an hour ago. In fact, my headache was just a dull thumping now, and if I didn't know better, I'd say that the more I talked to Kay, the less pain I felt. Wouldn't that be something, me being able to transfer that horrible headache to someone just by talking? What if my monkeys were escaping and running straight to Kay? Then the worst thought, did I care?

I hadn't invited her over to sit here. I wasn't the one that started chatting away about their entire life to a perfect stranger. Granted, she did buy me a coffee in exchange for my time, but she and I weren't going to be friends when this was all over with, were we? I'd never see her again, and here I would be, walking around with a little bit of her and her story forever. It wasn't likely I would forget this encounter. That's what happens, I sit and talk with you, and you're a part of me from that moment on, but what if this part of me had to stick with her? Is the lack of extended connection enough for me to keep going? She couldn't blame me for her pain later. She didn't even know my last name. Handing over my pain to a complete stranger, did I have it in me? What's worse, how far am I willing to take it?

Not even realizing it, here I was still talking away to Kay while I sat contemplating what I'd do if any of this were real. I had been telling a story about a book I had just finished reading how the characters had been expecting to go on and live happily ever after. Kay's face in a twisted smile at the thought, but the pain pulling at her edges, not letting her enjoy it as much as she might like. It was almost as if she were fading, the pain too much for her older body to handle, too much for her to take on completely. I couldn't stop, each word erupting out of my mouth faster than the last. Each monkey was grabbing a parachute and diving headfirst out of the plane as if their entire existence depended upon it.

Once it was clear what was happening, it wasn't that I couldn't stop. It was that I didn't want to. I didn't care anymore about my headache, and if it might come back, I didn't care about anyone around me. What I needed now was to see what would happen, and as I watched the first drip fall onto her shirt and the crimson stain spread, a sense of wonderment, fear, but most of all, power overcame me. It's sometimes strange the person you find out you could be in the span of a conversation. My headache is gone now, and Kay crumpled comfortably in her chair. It was time to go. I had errands to run.

Jenny Leidecker

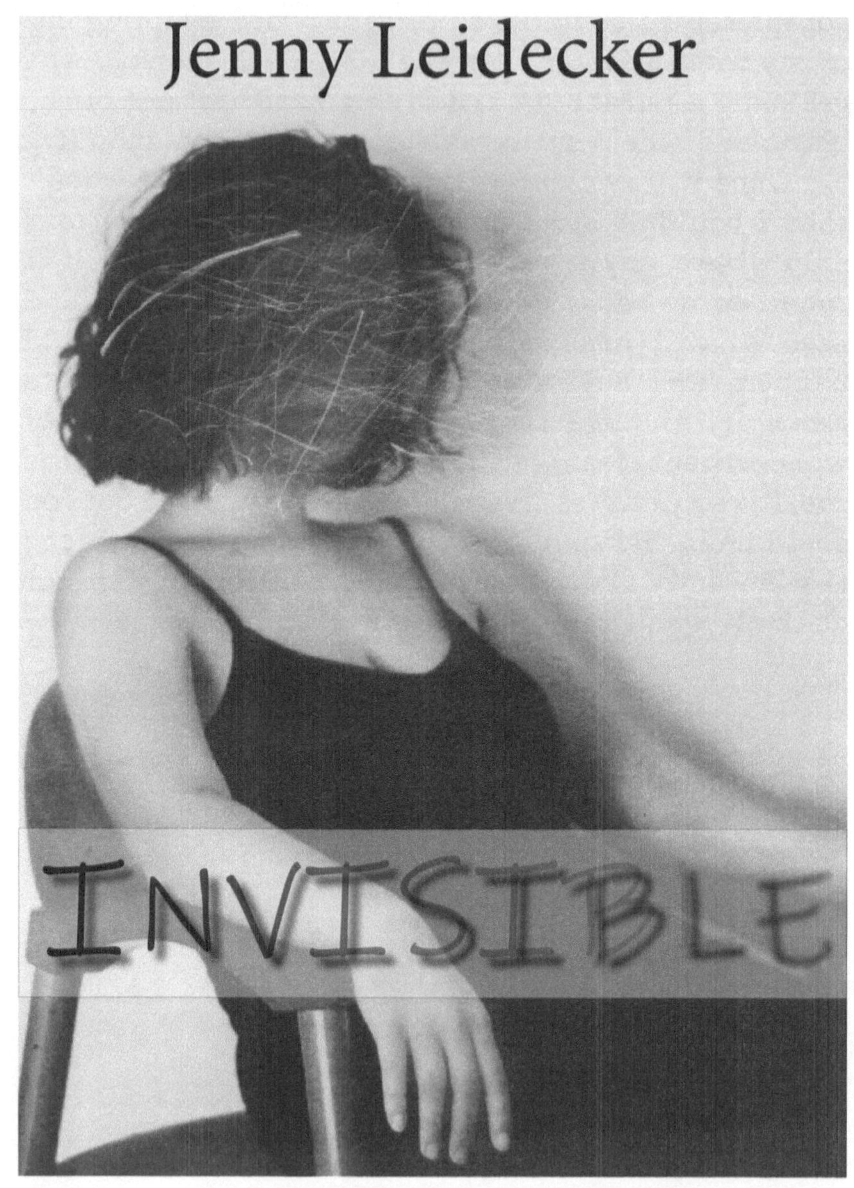

INVISIBLE

ONE

Do you remember the moment you disappeared? The moment you ceased to exist in the way you thought you did in the world. The minute you were no longer real or yourself, but just a figment of someone's imagination. I remember precisely when I vanished from the world, although, looking back at it now, I had slowly been fading for months without even knowing it. It's a unique space to exist, that small place just between the living and unseen. I've been here for a while now, my perpetual limbo, not sure what I should be doing or if I could get away with doing nothing. Is that when I'd become visible to those around me again, or would I fade into oblivion from that moment on?

I think it starts when you're addressed only as "honey," "sweetie," "Ms.," "dear," or "ma'am"; you get to the point where you're not sure anyone knows your real name anymore. Existing as a pack mule for those around you, carrying their keys, or toys, and all their emotional baggage and disappointment that they hand over all too willingly for you to hold onto instead. Turning from it all and walking away like they're free to live their lives without a burden or care in the world, because now you own it, and well, who cares if you take care of it, that is until they ask for it back. Of course, they don't want it back to heal from it or to unpack it. No, they want to use it against you or someone else or use it as an excuse for why they are who they are. In that instance, you go from being a storage container to an incompetent concierge that scratched their luggage or wasn't handling it all correctly, and not the way they would have. Once they've finished parading it around and gathering up their needed sympathy to cushion their bruised egos for the next extended span of time, they quickly toss it back in your direction. Leaving you again as the caretaker of their pain to drag around with your own until they snap their fingers in need of it again for their self-serving rituals they've become so proficient at performing. Strangely enough, they never consider holding onto any of it themselves. It's no fun to keep the blame, so much better to share it with the person you've forced it onto in the first place.

That's me, only there when needed and only for a blink of an eye, maybe a full breath, but then poof, gone again. After a while in this space, you start to wonder what you could get away with, if anything. Well, maybe you wouldn't have that thought, but I sure did. It started small to see if I solidified in front of people or not. My experiment was beginning close to home, around family and friends. Small gatherings where I was rarely engaged in any of the conversations, existing only to keep the children occupied and out of the way of the rest of the adults enjoying themselves. I could sit there with them all and be just as invisible as the air around them. The first couple of times, I didn't press my luck. I just needed to see if there was a boundary line that if I crossed it, someone might see me again. I'd take little things from the table and blatantly put them in my bag. I had accumulated a lighter, some fruit, a deck of cards, and even a small decorative bowl from my sister's living room. That one I took while two people looked right at me, or I should say, right through me. Not one of them batting an eye as I pulled it from the shelf, walked to my bag, and sat it inside. Completely invisible. I didn't know whether to be angry or amazed anymore.

Then I needed to push my experiment out into the world. How far could I take this now? I was just as much of a wisp of smoke everywhere else, and the question as to, do I really exist, walked through my mind often. Have you ever thought that maybe you were a figment of your own imagination? That perhaps you really didn't exist at all, and you were only floating through reality as a spectator or a ghost, just realized enough to benefit those around you but never fully formed in a way to make a difference or accomplish anything. I would become angrier with each thought of how little people saw me, how little I was allowed to exist in my own life, and what did my life even look like anymore?

I started to become more brazen in these activities of mine. I accumulated random objects from places I had to go often, places where people should have known me or at least recognized that I was a regular there. My hairdresser didn't even bother learning my name, and I had been seeing her for over two years now. When she addressed the woman behind me by her name and told her she was glad she decided to come back, I didn't feel bad about the new bottle of shampoo and conditioner I walked out with that afternoon. I didn't even bother to put them in my bag, just straight out the door with one in each hand. She'd never be able to remember who I was to stop me even if she did see me. I had turned into a common thief, and no one noticed, nor did they seem to care.

It's funny; I never even considered what I would do or say if someone caught me. I think I knew that they never would, that this experiment was just confirmation of the truth I already knew. So, why bother trying to hide it anymore. I didn't need a mask over my face. I was already faceless. Taking these things from people and places didn't make me feel any better. It only irritated me more, and my thoughts on what to do next looked a little darker when I stared into the mirror. What scared me the most wasn't the thought; it was how easily I recognized myself there in the darkness. It felt cozy and warm; it felt like home.

INVISIBLE

TWO

I contemplated for days as to how far I might be willing to go. Maybe I could take over someone's identity and become realized for a while, but then what fun would that be? This land of thievery wasn't all that enjoyable either, and it wasn't like I could rob a bank or anything. I might be invisible to the rest of the world, but what an inconvenient superpower when you know that you are never invisible to the security cameras. Those random eyes in the sky were the only proof that I did exist. They kept me from doing anything too crazy, for a while anyway. I had to remember those little truth-sayers when out in public. I could never disappear from them. They would always see me.

As the all and none of the above at the same time in my world, I ran too many errands to count for everyone other than me, it seemed. Picking up new shoes here for one, dry cleaning there for another, and ensuring the well-being of all those involved at any given moment, but never concerned with my own. The enamel began to wear down more and more each day as I watched my life push through the rest of the world's existence and never having one of my own. The anger building into rage, and I didn't worry too much about it until the dreams began. Waking in the morning with a smile spread across my face as I recall the blood smeared into my clothes.

They started small, dreaming of randomly tripping someone in the street and watching as they never noticed I was there-a ghost of the real world. Over the weeks, they progressed quickly, from random assaults to the first time I entered REM with a weapon. I shocked myself after waking up. Not only had I liked it, but I found myself contemplating the details. I considered all the possibilities as to how I'd do it. Who would it be? Where? The idea consumed me for days and weeks. I'd spend my time out in the world thinking of just what I would do, checking locations for cameras, watching people as they ordered their food or coffee, looking them up and down, and deciding if they were the one worthy of being my first.

Sometimes, I would dream of them, the woman in the coffee shop or the man at the grocery store, waking up in a haze of need and determination. They all were victims of my sadistic desires at least once, and every night I wallowed in the blood and fear of my target. The more I dreamt of it, the more I could taste it. I'd wake up with the smell of them still in my nose. I was obsessed, and I had never wanted anything more than this. I dealt with the occasional moment of doubt, thinking there was something wrong with me for considering such things and trying to convince myself of how wrong it was, but then I'd return to my moment of clarity and be right back gripped by my thoughts. They began to dominate every part of my life. I'd imagine all the different ways I could pull the life from them, searching for my style, my niche, I suppose.

As I watched their existence fade from their eyes every night, in that moment, they finally would see me. The last person they would look upon as they disappeared into oblivion just as I had. The truth is, had they seen me in the first place, they would have been safe from my sudden materialization within their lives, but they never did. My compassion for the rest of the world was dissipating as I evaporated from the world around me, and my presence less and less real with each passing day.

I truly had become a ghost in my own life. I noticed as the requests for me to do things waned, I was just a functioning cog and no longer a thought to anyone. I'd go to the coffee shop, and the girl at the counter waiting there to take my order would pretend like I wasn't there, like she couldn't see me, and I started to believe maybe I wasn't there at all. Never getting my order taken, I'd grab the next person's coffee and head out to do what was needed from me that day. I began to wonder if I had died and just never knew it, had I ceased to exist altogether? Of course, the making of dinner and watching others enjoy it without a word to me curbed that thought fairly quickly. That would have been something, though, a ghost with a desire to hurt and kill someone, dreaming about it, obsessing about it; I'm sure there's a story about something like that out there somewhere, but this isn't one. Too bad, it definitely would have made the planning process a hell of a lot easier. Oh well, maybe in my next life, or afterlife.

Weeks turned into months of me grinding my teeth and silently raging at how little my life mattered and at how there was even less I could do about it. I had killed more than half the town in my mind and in my dreams, not one of them ever knowing or ever seeing me for that matter. Then there's that moment, that instance when dreams and thoughts mingle with the real world, and you're not sure if you're asleep or awake any longer. Standing in line at the corner store, I could see the security camera feed on the screen behind the lady there ringing up the man in front of me, but there was no me. It wasn't possible, and I moved closer to the counter, thinking maybe I was just out of the frame, but nothing. I pinched myself to see if I was dreaming and if I was, my subconscious and I were going to discuss how standing in line to check out a package of toilet paper was not how I wanted to spend my dream time. Feeling the twinge of pain as I grabbed at my upper arm and squeezed, I dropped the package in my hand and froze as the thoughts swirled around like a tornado destroying the reality of what had been before and clearing the way to build something completely different, a world I controlled. What did it even mean now? And I couldn't help but smile at all the possibilities that lay in front of me. Where did I even start?

INVISIBLE

THREE

It amazed me as I stood there paying for my toilet paper that the woman ringing me up never looked at me once. She saw my item, and I swiped my card through the reader to pay, and as she set my receipt on the counter, she didn't see me at all. She turned to the man next in line, who had started moving forward before I had an opportunity to step away from the counter. I was nobody to anybody, and as I looked back at the camera feed on the screen once more, I was nobody to anything as well. I ceased to exist in that instance, and I knew right then that this was the final sign I had been waiting to see, for me to be completely and fully invisible to the entire world.

For a moment, I considered it to be a fluke, my minds-eye playing tricks on me, only showing me what I had hoped to see and not the reality. I couldn't possibly go out and do whatever I wanted just because I didn't see myself in one camera. This theory needed testing that needed to be confirmed before I could genuinely believe I didn't exist anymore. That's not right, is it? People are expecting me to do the things I usually do, aren't they? I don't know, and honestly, I don't know what I don't know, and that was the most frustrating of all of it.

Here we are again, back at square one, and I don't know where to begin. How do I test this hypothesis of nonexistence, and what qualifies to prove the affirmative? Have I just gone mad and started to hallucinate all of this? The anger I had been building up over the last few months was enough to have pushed me over the edge. It was more than enough to have created in me some false reality that I now believed to be true. I knew that was a possibility, and it scared me that I might never know the difference again. What if I had been lost in my own mind, circling my hate for so long, that I was no longer present in my daily life? What if me not feeling seen wasn't true at all, and that I had actually been engaging in conversations with these people all along and only a part of me retreated to that dark corner of my mind, alone and unseen and full of dark thoughts and desires? That was more petrifying than fading from existence was. That felt more permanent, more terrifying than just vanishing did. My padded cell that no one knew existed, much less how to get me out of it or if I even wanted them to in the first place.

I could get away with the thought of retreating into my seclusion. That wasn't abnormal, was it? It was this new need of pain and death that had wrapped its hand around my throat, holding me hostage from anything else in the world, and the only way to breathe again would be to provide this desideratum with it's required sacrifice. I don't know how I got here, but I know how to get out. That's not true. There's no doubt within me that if I kneel at this altar, then my conversion will be complete. Offering faith to the faithless wrapped in such a package filled with understanding and acceptance is enough to convert those in search of something bigger than themselves. Add in a purpose, and you've sold the masses, but in this instance, I was the masses, and my task was of my own devising, one I had created out of anger and frustration. It didn't make it any less holy, any less sanctified. What it did make it was mine.

I had no misconceptions either; I could easily take the life of someone else. What did their lives mean anyway if we could so easily fade into the nothingness without anyone paying attention as we disappear? Imprinted on people's memory like a faded photograph, only able to make out a few details here and there but the moment lost, fallen into the crevices of our mind to be brought out by a familiar sound or smell, and even then, still not sure what you're reaching for. Your fingers are grasping at smoke, trying to catch just a second of reality, only to watch it all fade away before you knew what it was in the first place. That's all it boiled down to, the striking of a match, with your memory dissipating as quickly as the smoke lifting from that spot you once stood on fire with life.

Now don't get me wrong, some people were there to light the fire of others, and they made their mark on their lives; those people didn't just fade. Their flame carried on one by one to anyone who had ever been around them. That, however, wasn't me. I was more like that dud match that had gotten wet, and no matter how long you let it dry out, it became a crumbly mess when you tried to strike it. No smoke to fade away, just the brokenness of an almost existence in pieces on the table, quickly swept onto the floor and forgotten. I had accepted this long ago and watched in true spectator fashion as the pieces of my life swept out of the way of those more important than I was. Well, not anymore. I had spent the last few months dreaming of death and pain, watching the life drain from those who didn't know how quickly that fire could burn out until I showed them. Each one showing me more and more how badly I wanted it. I don't think in all my life I had ever felt such focus and ambition to do something as I did this, but first, how to determine if I've become a ghost in my own life or if I've just gone crazy thinking now, I'm some invisible person, so let's start a killing spree. I'd put my money on both, but is a little insane all that bad? I mean, maybe.

INVISIBLE

FOUR

I pondered for a day or two on just how to test what could and could not be considered reality anymore. I stopped doing things here and there, and the world went on as usual, as if I had never existed at all. I should have been more upset than I was, but it only deepened my smile as I found myself weaving in and out of the world unnoticed. Grabbing someone else's coffee at my favorite shop, walking in and pulling food directly from the display without anyone bothered by my presence, and as far as any of them were concerned, I wasn't present; I wasn't there at all.

Life just floated by hour by hour now, and I needed less and less sleep as the planet spun through its daily routine. That's one thing I didn't have anymore, no routine to follow, no errands, no one concerned as to where I was or what I was doing. I had become less than a memory. It was as if I had never been born, that life had never pumped through my veins in the first place, and maybe it hadn't. Perhaps all I had ever been was a wisp of smoke, only believing I once had purpose when I had never been anything more than a conscious thought aware of others and blind to my own lack of reality.

I couldn't believe that, and I knew if I did, I'd vanish completely. I wanted to enjoy myself and these moments in the shadows. What little sleep I had was filled with the same dark and twisted themes, each one growing more vivid. I began to feel their skin against my hands, and their pulse slows as they sputtered to gain a mouthful of air as I wrapped my fingers tighter around their necks. I could feel their bodies relax as the blood poured from the wound I had inflicted, almost as if they were slowly drifting to sleep in my arms. Every dream was drawing me closer to the real thing, closer to the desire to see and feel it there at my own hands. To watch the transubstantiation of their sacrifice, becoming the nourishment of my soul.

The fantasy struggling to find reality was having to put up less of a fight each day. I had walked in front of every camera I could find, looked directly into them as I took things, trying to see if the electronic eye could see me. I even went as far as standing in the middle of the police station with a sign in hand and facing their cameras, not to mention the officer on duty there at the front with a poster that read, "I'm going to kill someone." I suppose if that doesn't get someone's attention, nothing will. That was the final test, the last option I could think of that could stop me from acting on these ever-present impulses that were now taking over my every thought. All that was left was to act on them, and for a split second, I second-guessed myself. I thought better of it and knew this was my point of no return. Either

I would be resolute in my decision to move forward or walk away altogether. That last ounce of doubt I left there on the chair with my poster, it was time to decide who would be first because I knew they would not be the last.

INVISIBLE

FIVE

She didn't know I was there. Hell, no one had known I was around for months, but soon she would wish she had seen me, had sensed me around her. I had thought for a long time how I would go about this the first time. I didn't want something I could use from a distance, like a gun. I wanted something up close, something personal. I wanted to feel them in my hands and watch as they slowly dissolved out of existence. I wanted to know if they would see me before the light dimmed and extinguished behind their eyes. I needed to watch them and feel them as they died.

She had been sitting there at the coffee shop alone, her head in a book. She was completely unaware of the world around her. I had seen her there many times, always the same routine during each visit. She'd order a large sugar-filled coffee, curl up in one of the chairs in the corner and sip on it for a few hours while she read her book. At least three times a week, I'd see her there, and not once was she interrupted by another person or her phone ringing. I don't think I ever saw her receive a text or look at her phone, for that matter. It was almost as if she was invisible in her own way over there in that corner. No one to reach out to her or to walk over and make small talk, but by the looks of the smile on her face, she enjoyed her life just as it was. It's good that she had been so happy, or apparently happy during her short life, because that was all she'll know now. I think that's why I picked her to be the first, how content and genuinely happy she seemed to be from afar. A life snuffed out during its prime, but also without too many regrets. It's difficult to be that happy if you're dragging around an abundance of pain or guilt. She would die happy.

Don't get me wrong, there was going to be some pain and fear as well, but overall, she'd die happy. Not that it was going to matter to me too much, I had already decided her fate. I had gone and sat across from her about a week ago, pulled her wallet out of her bag, and found her address. I think that's when you know you can't get caught, sitting there rummaging through someone's bag and digging through their wallet right before their eyes and not once receiving so much as a side-eyed glance. Writing it down, I had left and went to check it out. No pets, which I had found odd. I expected at least one cat to be curled up in the corner somewhere, but nothing but a small goldfish on the table by the door. Those types of commitments sure did make it easier to sit in a coffee shop for hours on end for sure.

The rest of the apartment was what you'd expect to find. There were books everywhere, no sign of many if any guests having been there, and not too many photos of family scattered across the shelves either. I began to wonder how long it would be for anyone to notice she wasn't floating in and out of their lives anymore. A pang of sadness and understanding swirled around my heart for a moment, and then it was gone. There was a reason I had found this woman. She was placed in front of me to be the first. She was a part of my life I had seen before, she was familiar, and had we met prior to my vanishing, we could have easily been friends. Looking closer at the books on the shelves, I noticed titles I had read many times and a few I had hoped to get to at some point years ago and never did. Ambition and passion are placed on the shelf, waiting to find their home somewhere along the way, but never quite getting there. Yes, she was familiar, and the memories of my early adult life rushed through my mind as I weaved my way in and around her apartment. She'd never see the struggle of the adult life she hadn't made it to just yet, and she'd never know what it would feel like to disappear in such a way like I did. Forever young and perpetually happy, a life stopped at its pinnacle, that's the gift I was giving her. She'd never know to feel grateful. She'd never know what I could be saving her from in the end.

Watching her now from across the room, I waited as she read the last few lines of her book and closed it with a smile, content in the ending written just as it should be. Just like hers, only she didn't know it yet. No understanding of how today would be the last day she'd relax with a cup of coffee, the last time she would read that last line. It's almost poetic, completing the one story she could flip the final page of and landing upon that last word seeing how perfectly it all came together with a final period. Today I would be that punctuation on the final page of her life. I would be the end.

She got up to leave, and I followed her home. I knew the turns she would have to make and the time it would take to get there. I had made this walk before. Never once did she look back at me behind her. Not once did she recognize the reaper that she was bringing home. As she walked through the front door, I pushed past the frame and into the living room. Like a phantom, I stood there only a few steps from her as she leaned down and sprinkled a few flakes into the goldfish bowl. She smiled and moved about, setting her bag on the counter, and shelving the book she had only just finished. I didn't look at the title, it was her last story, not mine, and it belonged to her alone. I was here now, and there was no stopping the series of events that were going to take place, and every step I took closer to her was only another last moment for her.

I made sure she was close enough to the wall, and when I found myself face to face with her, I could see the joy behind her eyes. She exhaled a smile, and before she could take another step, she was in my hands. Arms flailing in response to my hands wrapped tightly around her throat, and I walked her back into the wall. Pinning her back, I forced all of my weight against her and slowly added more pressure. Her eyes wide in disbelief, still unable to see me, but I was a witness to the fear. Watching as the unknown took control and held her life in its hands. I was that darkness, the unseen death that had chosen her and set this as the appointed time on her calendar marked, "last breath." I could feel her pulse as it slowed, and it felt like a whispered secret that I held in the palm of my hands. As she begged the air to find her lungs, each attempt only found my fingers tighter than they were just a second before. The time was close. I could feel it, her body feeling heavier as her legs faltered beneath her, unable to hold the weight of her existence any longer. Her eyes shut tight, trying to wake up from the nightmare she'd found herself in, and when she opened them for the last time, I was there.

There was no doubt that I had materialized before her in an instant, and the fear and confusion hit all at once before that last second of life, then there was understanding, a moment of clarity, and a chosen release. With that, the joy that had been illuminated in her eyes faded, turning her into the next memory for those who would try to hold onto who she had been and the wisps of smoke she had managed to leave in her wake for them to reach for whenever they thought of her.

As she slid to the floor, a puddle of a person, stepping back, I felt peace. Complete and connected in a way I had never felt before, and as I walked out the door, I felt free in a way I had never understood. I turned to look at her one last time, inhaling the air that would never fill her lungs again, and with a smile, I was gone.

INVISIBLE

SIX

I felt lighter as I walked away, almost as if my feet no longer touched the ground. I could still feel her pulse at my fingertips and that last look in her eyes would be with me forever. It was glorious. I felt like I had been waiting my entire life to feel this free and in control of what I was, even if that meant I was a monster. I had watched every last second of that woman's life as if slid from this existence into the next, whatever that may be. I had determined the beginning of the end, I had taken it, and it was mine.

My indoctrination into this new religion was now complete, and I knelt at the alter waiting for my next holy task to be shown to me. I would worship now until I achieved sainthood, devout and unquestioning of the belief I now held tight. Unwavering until the end and cleansed of my uncertainty. I knew if I stepped into the light, I could never turn away again.

I replayed it over and over again in my mind for what had to be days, but I paid no attention to the passing of time any longer. I rarely slept and I barely ate; and I couldn't remember the last time I felt tired or hungry. I was fueled by the need, that compulsion to feel the life drain from another body once again. I had seen her before, but this time was different, this time I knew it was her. It had been a few months maybe, the days no longer mattering, and I wasn't sure how long it had been since this all began anyway. When I had seen her the first time, she was happy, almost floating through life, and now she beamed. She was a lighthouse, and I was lost at sea in search of the next shore. She was leading me directly to safety, at the cost of her existence.

Walking over to where she sat there in the library, I could see all of her books and notebooks spread out. College courses on history and composition, and notebooks with hearts and initials drawn all across them. How the hell did I get to the library? It doesn't matter, nothing else matters now but her. She was here to rescue me, and I was here prepared to worship at the alter once more.

I hadn't thought this one through; I hadn't taken any time to plan what I would do, but I knew just how she would become the next sacrifice. Her heart was full, and her thoughts in the clouds, she was in love. What a perfect moment to freeze, that lost and longing feeling lasting for eternity, never to be marred by time. That was my gift to her. Freeing her from the possibility of pain and hurt, who wouldn't want that life? I should say, who wouldn't want that death? Want it or not, I was here to offer it with a no returns policy attached, and as she gathered her things to leave, I pulled the letter opener off the librarian's desk and followed her out. She stood waiting for the bus, and I breathed in the faint smell of flowers surrounding her. I can almost picture the bouquet placed at the center of her table with a card attached and marked, "with love." I was here to fulfill that sentiment, this was a gift made out of love, one she'd never get an opportunity to thank me for.

We filed onto the bus, and she stepped all the way to the very back row, and I took up the seat next to her, not that she noticed. I waited to see how long of a ride we might have, and once she pulled out her pen and began doodling on the cover of her notebook, I knew there was time. Time to savor each drop as it slowly poured from her, just as her love poured from the tip of her pen now. Holding onto the letter opener, I lunged towards her and watched as it skimmed across her body. It was if I was only partially there, and the force I had attempted only landed with half the strength. I felt as if I had been fading not just from the world around me, but from existence myself. Angered by the thought, I ground my teeth and lunged harder and felt as the metal pierced her skin there between her ribs. The shock causing her to jump in her seat, and as I pulled the intrusion from her side, the life that filled her began to stain her shirt and puddle onto the seat beside her. As she went to stand, I held her in place and for the first time, she felt trapped. That recognizable look of fear in her eyes as she searched for a reason.

I sat back in my seat and observed as she opened her mouth in a silent scream, unable to push out any sound, the blood filling her lung instead of the air she so desperately needed. No one paid her any attention, and I had a front row seat to the end. Her breathing ragged and for a second, there was sorrow in her eyes, the knowing that there will never be another thought given in love but this last one. With that final thought, she looked up and saw me. Truly saw the devotion to her memory in my eyes, and a thousand questions sprang from hers in an instant. Not one of them to be answered, only my prayer of the preservation of her innocence in love, and with a final amen, she was gone. Every drop of love poured out from her body, and forever at peace.

As the bus stopped and I walked away from her, I remembered to smile once again.

INVISIBLE

SEVEN

I didn't remember anything for a while after I stepped off the bus. I felt the world move around me, but I barely remembered taking a step. My body felt as if it was floating, not fully formed, and only my thoughts were realized when I considered them. I was here but not, gone, but present, and even I hadn't seen myself in so long, I wasn't sure I was real anymore. I don't know what kept me tethered to this world, but whatever it was, it wasn't ready to let go just yet.

Standing there on the street corner that I had zero recollection of how I managed to end up on, but here I was, nonetheless. I didn't have a clue where I was going, or if I had even been heading anywhere, to begin with, so I just stood there as the people filtered around me. I kept trying to grasp at a thought, to find some direction as to where my destination was. Everyone else seemed to know where they were going, determined steps filled with purpose, and here I was lost, not even sure which foot to put in front of the other anymore.

I watched as the light turned green and the sea of people surrounded me again, waiting for the impending "don't walk" sign to give them access to the rest of their day. An inconvenience they couldn't be bothered with any longer as the tension built all around me. Dozens of pulled rubber bands are waiting to launch to the other side with a momentum unmatched by my own. I was barely moving in any direction at the moment, much less forward, and then I noticed her there on the very edge of the curb. She was going to spring from it at any moment, and I worked my way closer to her. I could see it written all over her. She was important in her own life and successful at what she did, a force to those around her. She was all the things I had never been, my opposite and my envy in a pair of heels.

I shouldn't be jealous. I'd managed to accomplish more of what I wanted since I vanished from those around me than I ever did in the years before. I had succeeded in fulfilling my dreams of sort, but she had lived, she had a purpose, and I wanted it, and short of that, I wanted it to disappear just as I had. It was still a gift, pulling her from the world at the height of her success, giving her no opportunity to fail. She'd be lifted up from those who had known her as one they hoped to be in time, a martyr of ambition. Yes, it would be a gift, and it would be one I'd wrap in a bow and hand to her.

As the thought finished forming, the answer to the question was picking up speed and heading our way. I reached out to push her, but my hands never made contact. I tried again, but I couldn't connect, and I realized I couldn't remember the last time I had felt anything. The anger and frustration started to boil over, and the pain of losing myself erupting from my soul forced out a scream that pierced through my world into hers, and as she twisted to see the source, her heel slipped from the curb, and she fell forward. In an instant, she was gone.

Do you remember the moment you disappeared?

LUCKY
Jenny Leidecker

LUCKY

I like to consider myself a good person, at least most of the time. Honestly, what does that even mean? Good is subjective, isn't it? I guess I should say that I do my best to treat people kindly and with respect, but deep down, there's a part of me that just doesn't give a shit. We all have that, though, or at least I think we do. Life just sort of goes on by; there's nothing spectacular here. I'm an ordinary person in an ordinary job, and there isn't anything I can think of that's special about me. The type of person you wouldn't look at twice if we were in the same room or in line together. Just ordinary. I think I've said that already. Anyway.

I've liked my life this way. No spotlight to draw any attention to me, or accolades of any note to even warrant a line in the local newspaper. I've kept under the radar, just existing. I prefer it that way. It seems like an awful lot of trouble to have to deal with the acknowledgment or celebrity of a situation. I don't need that, and lord knows, I don't want it either. So, what manner of sorcery managed to convince me to buy that Lucky 7's scratch-off the other day is beyond me, but I did, and now I don't know what to do with any of it.

I can't recall any time I've ever won anything, especially not off one of those scratchers. Hell, I've even played bingo a couple of times and left worse off than when I started, that's for sure. I couldn't even enjoy it, was too focused on trying to win somehow, but it's all chance. Like they say, you just need a little luck. Well, that's one thing that's been elusive my entire life. I couldn't even manage to get lucky enough to ever win at drawing straws. I think my brothers and sister figured that one out long ago and knew that no matter the job, I'd be stuck with it. They didn't even break a sweat after a while, and in the end, we quit playing those eenie meenie games to see who was running off to tell mom all the wrong that had just happened. It also meant that I was the one dealt most of the punishment for it too. So, as you see, there are several reasons why I don't chance it, because chances are guaranteed that I'm going to lose.

That wasn't the case the other day, though. Like I said, not even sure what made me look in the direction of those things, but the gold glitter on that seven caught my eye and wouldn't let me go. It was almost as if I had been hypnotized by the sparkle on that green card, all covered in four-leaf clovers. You have to know they're trying to sell the luck if you're gonna toss those things all over something. Never found one of them either, although I'm pretty sure everyone else in my family did at some point. My sister even wrapped hers up in scotch tape and carries it around in her coin purse everywhere she goes. I thought about taping one together myself, you know, creating my own luck, but it would have likely just backfired on me in the end. No need to channel anything extra in that bad category, and tempting fate never sounds like a good idea. At least not to me.

There I was, though, sitting in my car staring at that glittery green and gold ticket, thinking what I always thought. My bad luck was compounded. Not only was I not going to win, but I'd wasted the couple of dollars on it in the first place. I might as well have laid that money on the counter, set it on fire, and watched as it burned right there in front of the cashier instead. I might have actually enjoyed that option more than scratching off this mess to find I'm just a loser twice today. At least staring at the flames would have been some kind of entertainment. Pulling out the coin to reveal what I already knew didn't just seem like a lost cause, but torture. Why in the world had I been such an idiot to think anything was going to change. My bad luck or lack of good luck, however you want to frame it was absolute. It never wavered, and it always won, unlike me.

I'm constantly the scapegoat for karma to even out the universe. I'm the one that keeps the scales from tipping too far in favor of the fortunate, even if it never tilts in my direction. Here I was again, knowing the next person in line who bought one of these was likely going to win the $10,000 jackpot almost made me sick to my stomach and wonder if I should just go in and tempt fate for the first time to see if maybe it could be me. I knew it wouldn't, but today for some reason, I felt the need to have a little, I don't know what you'd call it. Faith?

Either way, it was time to see what was behind this tacked-on glitter. I scratched off the first box, and of course, it was a seven. That's how they get your heart pounding a bit. That way, if you don't win, you felt like you were so close to it, you're willing to try again next time that glittery seven catches your eye. My heart doesn't do that; it just wallows in constant disappointment. I learned a long time ago only to get worked up when it was time for a physical at the doctor or trying to cross a busy street. Either of those events, and you'd think I was about to be crowned Miss Universe or inherit millions of dollars. Neither of those were ever going to happen for numerous reasons, but the chance of a poor health report or being struck by some rouge car in a freak accident of human Frogger, those were more up my alley of possibilities.

I scratched off the second box and tried to guess the random number I would find there, probably a zero. That'd be the most fitting anyway. As I revealed more, another seven lay there, and my face twisted in disbelief and anger at the meanness involved in such a trick. What wretched person thought it was alright to play such a horrible game with someone's emotions this way. Obviously, not mine, but that's only because I know how this is all going to end. Next comes the zero, that number reminding the person left holding the useless ticket just what they're worth. Well, the jokes on them, I've known that one for years. This was not about to be some life lesson in failure for me, just my part in saving someone else the heartache of feeling so close to winning only to have the rug pulled from under their feet in one sudden motion.

Might as well get it over with, just like ripping

off a bandaid. As I scratched off the last bit of glitter to reveal the last number concealed beneath it, my hand began to shake. That wasn't a zero. In fact, if I didn't know any better, I would have thought it was going to be another seven, but that's not possible. This is me we're talking about, and there's no way this bit of paper will be the catalyst to disrupt the natural order of things. I'm the one who loses, never the one who wins. I can't even imagine what that would look like in real life. How do you win? It's not something I've ever experienced before, and I was certain it wasn't something I was going to experience now.

As the last number stood there staring at me in jest, I flipped it over to read the disclaimer. Surely, I'd bought one of those trick tickets that you give family for their birthday or holidays, making them think they've won the prize, only to find out it was all a rouse. My whole life had been one of those, a cruel joke thinking there was some value attached to what I had and what I was, only to read the disclaimer to see it was all worthless in the end. But this wasn't the end, and this wasn't a joke. Those three sevens glaring at me on this ticket seemed like a mistake, like the universe and karma had forgotten who I was all of a sudden and left me holding the winning ticket. It wasn't natural, but one more look down, and I had to admit, somehow, it was real. I had won. It was impossible, but it had happened, and my hands shook so hard I could barely make out the numbers for a minute. I flipped it back over to read what I was supposed to do next.

I couldn't comprehend language anymore. Couldn't string the words together into a coherent sentence, much less understand any of it. I shoved the ticket under my thigh, scared I'd somehow lose it if it wasn't tacked down. I still needed to be touching it so that it didn't fly out the window or someone reach in and grab it from me. Now that would be my luck, and I was enjoying this overwhelming feeling a little too much to give it up any time soon. Taking a few deep breathes, I allowed myself to settle and try to calm down long enough to read what the hell I'm supposed to do next. I'm going to guess if I walk into this corner store, they're not going to have ten thousand dollars sitting there waiting just to hand over to me either. Seriously, ten thousand dollars, what am I even going to do with that? Smiling to myself, I spent it ten thousand times in my mind in a matter of seconds. I knew for a fact it was going to be there and gone quickly, but just the idea that it would exist at all was nearly a miracle, to me anyway.

Having a moment to relax and pulling the ticket out from its hiding space, I half expected it to reveal different numbers all together, but it didn't. They were still there, and I was, for the first time, a winner. Maybe after so many years, my luck was turning around. Now that would be something. Flipping to the back, I had two options, mail it in, not a chance, or take it to a lottery center. Didn't know where one of those were, but I was going to find out here pretty quick. Grabbing a pen from the console, I filled out my name and address on the back, and I had to stop several times to shake the tremors from my fingers to make sure it was legible. The last line required a signature, and I stared at it for what seemed like a minute too long. What was I waiting for? Just sign the damn thing and claim it? My hand trembled again as I pressed the pen against the paper. Taking one last deep breath, I watched as my name slowly appeared, one letter at a time drawn out across that last bit of blank space.

I hadn't realized I had been holding my breath, but I was, and as I exhaled, it all felt different. I can't explain it, but something had definitely changed. With a quick swirl of a pen, I wasn't a loser anymore; suddenly, I was a winner for the first time ever. I wasn't about to press my luck and instead pulled on my seatbelt and backed out of my space. I was on high alert now. This little bit of luck I had found was going to come at a cost. I just knew it, and I didn't want to take any chances that it'd be at the expense of my car or my own bodily harm, for that matter. I could see me getting on the road and totaling my vehicle, leaving this newfound wealth to cover only part of a new one and actually catapulting me into debt instead. There are too many ways this could all go wrong, and at every turn, I'd think of a new one. I was too on edge to enjoy it fully yet. You get so used to the way things are supposed to go that when they suddenly change, you just don't know how to act, and I was acting like an idiot. Maybe this is what shock feels like because, without a doubt, I'm still stunned.

I drove straight to the lottery offices. I wasn't about to give this ticket the opportunity to change its spots and turn me back into a loser, not a chance. The closer I made my way there, the more I could feel the smile spread across my face. This was all a newfound feeling, and I'm not sure I've ever been this happy. Now, I'm not trying to say that having won a little money is what made me happy; that's not it at all. I think it's the idea that the world is spinning differently for me now or at least for once. I can claim this one. This one I won, and no one was going to believe it. Like I said, it's been the running theme throughout my life, and those around me had taken advantage of my misfortunes repeatedly. Some of them would purposefully invite me to events with raffles or those hideous casino nights, and they'd make sure to stand close enough to me to get the full effect of my possible good fortune escaping in fear that I might see it and hold onto it for myself. It never failed. If I were around, they'd all win, and of course, I'd do what I always do, lose. Well, not this time, not today, and I was going to grab my money and deposit it in the bank as quickly as possible. I can't take a chance that it somehow might disappear before my name is attached to it.

Carefully pulling into the parking lot and finding a spot far away from any other cars, I grabbed the ticket and held onto it inside my pocket. At least then, if it suddenly vanished, I'd know it. God help me if that happened. I think it might destroy me. I've had a taste of luck, of the fortune others had siphoned from me my entire life, and I didn't want to let it go. I couldn't help but think, don't let it disappear with each step as I walked across the parking lot. My own personal prayer for this reality to continue to exist.

I made it into the offices, and it felt like I had walked into a bank lobby. Just a couple of tellers against one wall and a receptionist there at the front to greet me. She gathered what I was there for and sent me off to one of the windows behind her. A robust woman in her forties stood behind the thick glass with the scowl of a DMV worker. I wonder how frustrating it must be to hand out money to people randomly that had accomplished nothing other than scratching off some colorful glue from a lottery ticket or to have somehow managed to pick just the right numbers that popped out of a ball machine on a Saturday night. Her job was the personification of my luck in this world until this very moment. Always giving out little bits here and there and never reaping the rewards herself. At that moment, I felt for her. I understood her.

I tried to tack on a knowing smile, to connect with her in some way, but the thick glass wouldn't allow for such things to make their way to her. I was just another lucky bastard as far as she was concerned, and the faster she got rid of me, the sooner she could quit thinking about it. The sooner she could stop seeing her misfortune staring back at her.

She was clinical about it all, not a single word of jest, and I tried hard to make her laugh. In the end, I felt like a stand-up comedian that had just bombed their worst set ever. My short stage career paid well, though. I walked out with a check in my name for ten grand. I'm still not sure how that's possible, and I began to consider for a second that maybe I was on the wrong career path but figured I wouldn't be paid in winning lotto tickets if I made it in front of a crowd. Another dream for another time, maybe.

I wrapped my hand around that check within my pocket even tighter than I had that winning ticket and carefully made my way back to my truck. Time moved at a glacier's pace, and you'd had thought I was nesting the most valuable Faberge egg in the world with the way I was walking. I had to look like a fool nearly tip-toeing my way across the asphalt, and truth be told, I didn't even consider someone robbing me. I just figured my luck would run out, and a piano would fall from the sky out of nowhere and onto my head at any moment. It didn't, and I think that might have been the final proof I needed that we were not living in a cartoon simulation either because if ever something massive was going to fall out of thin air and onto anyone, it would have been then, and it would have been me.

This day turned into a to-do list of tasks transporting this money from its original habitat into its new home and inside the comfort of my cozy, although empty bank account. I decided to walk it inside to the bank instead of through the drive-up window, finding myself more willing to face off with a bank robber than chance it with a strong gust of wind. I stood at the counter filling out the deposit slip and again found myself shaking off the nerves that were using my fingers to dance. However, it was when I went to endorse the back of the check that my breath caught again, and there seemed to be so much more attached to signing my name than it should have. Like somehow claiming it, I've taken on a new responsibility, a new curse.

That would have been my luck for sure, win some money only to find out it's the long-lost treasure of some cursed family making its way into my pocket and attaching the curse to me for all eternity. For a second, with that thought alone, I considered ripping the check to shreds at just the possibility. I didn't, but I sure did think about it. Here I was, another stop, another teller. This one, though, was all smiles. Of course, she was, I was handing her money, not expecting her to give me any in return, and basically, the transaction looked as if it amounted to nothing. Though it wasn't like I was giving it to her, or at least I didn't think I was, and I looked down quickly to reassess the deposit slip in my hand. It was my account number; I had checked it three times before feeling I had got it right. Smiling widely, she reached out her hand, and mine trembled as I let go of the only amount of luck I had ever possessed. Handing me back a receipt, it was done, and before I walked out the front door, I pulled up my account on my phone and stood stunned that the money was actually in there.

Now what? I had enough money to cover everything I needed. So, what did I want? I spent the next few hours contemplating exactly how I would spend my newfound fortune, but nothing seemed like it was worth it. There it was, my luck had found me again, or lack thereof, I should say. Here I was with what was basically a free ten thousand dollars, and I couldn't think of a damn thing to do with it. I was sure I would, but it was starting to make me anxious. What if I couldn't spend it fast enough on something I wanted and ended up stuck having to spend it on something I needed instead? I didn't want to have to need anything.

I jumped in my car and onto the road with the plan to go straight home before anything else took over my attention or the little nest of dollars that were hopefully getting cozy in my account.

Every light was green along the way, and I rarely, if ever, actually touched my brake as I drove home. This doesn't happen. My car has been so used to stopping at every single light since I took ownership of it that I can't even recount the number of times I've had to replace the pads and discs from the wear and tear. I'm not sure what Twilight Zone moment I'm having in my life, but I'm cautiously optimistic that maybe I've just finally run out of bad luck, and the only option left is good fortune. I mean, there has to be balance at some point, right?

There's nothing left to do but try and enjoy it, and that cliff-diving moment is enough to make me more nervous than I can remember being in a very long time. It doesn't feel right, this existence is not natural, and I don't know how to process any of it. Turning on the radio only to find my favorite song just starting, and the chills race up my back. It's all too good to be true, and I feel like I'm being conned out of something I wasn't aware I agreed to when I decided to be the target of some golden sparkle and lucky clovers.

Lost in a daydream of 'how is this happening,' I nearly miss my turn. I've never not been stopped at the light, and I wasn't paying enough attention to realize where I was. I've lived on that road for over ten years now, my faint green house on a dusty lot where the grass only grows in patches has been my home, and this has been my route to my front door for a decade. How did I nearly miss it? The steady flow of green lights and no need to slow down or stop keeping me transfixed on the forward momentum to the point I didn't know where I was or where I was going for a second.

Nearly screeching my tires to slow down enough to make the turn without flipping my car, I take control of the wheel and my speed as fast as possible. Luckily, there was no one there for me to hit. Now that's a thought, 'luckily,' that's not one I've used before. That all too good to be true feeling was returning and creeping up my spine as I closed in on my driveway. I didn't want to check my mail in fear that I'd find some poisonous snake leaping out at me or a letter from the IRS stating that I somehow owed them ten thousand dollars. I'd take on the snake any day over that last option.

I can't help but flinch, pulling down the door, but no snakes or bills of any kind meet me there. Not even a sliver of junk mail to be found, only a magazine I have a subscription for that I thoroughly enjoy. I'm smiling. I can't help myself; I'm actually smiling. It feels strange not to have the weight of that dark cloud that had been my companion all my life in my near vicinity; instead of some understanding that it was going to open up and pour down misfortune upon me at any moment, I felt warmth. The clouds had separated, and the sun was shining on me for the first time in as long as I could remember. I'm not sure I had ever felt this way before, and the spring in my step was new. I liked this feeling. Is this what other people feel throughout their lives? How could you ever be upset if you knew this feeling was out there to be had?

Walking up to the front door, a piece of paper had taped itself there. Here it was. Am I somehow being evicted from my own home? Each corner I turned causing me to question the length of my good fortune, as if it would all end in an instant. Honestly, the money could all disappear now that I'd found a drop of luck on my side. I didn't need it anymore. I felt lighter, freer than I've ever felt in my life. It was as if I had grasped some semblance of peace once I signed my name on the back of that ticket. My signature was buying me a new path to follow for the rest of my days. Somehow, I knew that even if the money disappeared, I'd be taken care of for the rest of my life. The struggle to enjoy and live each day was no longer holding me hostage, and instead, I had an easier way to walk from here on out. I could breathe without the weight of misfortune taking residence inside of me with each breath I took.

With a new sense of relief and purpose, the note barely mattered. Ripping it from the door and unfurling the message folded within, I find only kind words from my sister letting me know she was sorry that she had missed me and hoped I would give her a call when I made it back home. Of course, I would. I couldn't imagine anything more enjoyable than to end my afternoon with an impromptu visit with her. We were always there for each other growing up, and out of the three siblings I was tethered to in this life, she was the one that tried the hardest to push good fortune my way as we grew older.

Pulling out my phone, I flung a message in her direction and informed her that she was welcome to visit, and I'd even provide something to eat for added measure. Not that I felt like cooking, and as soon as she replied that she'd stop in, I picked up the phone and ordered a pizza. I was in too much of a good mood to find myself elbow deep in dirty dishes from cooking. I imagined that they both would arrive close to the same time, so I spent the next twenty minutes or so freshening up and changing clothes. I wanted to feel comfortable, and there was no reason to spend the rest of the night bound up in constrictive clothing when I had the ability to relax.

This was not typical of me. I would typically spend my entire day uncomfortable, and now sitting to think about it, some of that discomfort was of my own making. Doing things the hard way or not feeling worthy of relaxing, even in my own home. That all changed today, and I noticed more and more with each moment passing that maybe I had not been as unfortunate as I had made myself believe. Perhaps I had spent so much time feeling that I would always lose that I forced myself to be uncomfortable at every turn. What a disappointing thought. Had I really been creating my bad luck and misery? Surely not, at least not all of it. I couldn't have, but thinking on it more, it wasn't an impossible theory.

Just as I started to fall into a pool of self-doubt, the knock at the door pulled me back to shore, and I smiled again at how lucky I was to be stopped from such thoughts at just the right time. It's funny how you start to notice those types of things as you focus on the good things happening to you instead of the bad. That was my new goal in life, to keep an eye on the wonderful things going on and slowly start to ignore those instances of awfulness that always find their way into my every day. Who knew how easily I could change the thought process of my life with the purchase of a glitter-covered lotto ticket? Somehow those few dollars that I had been convinced I had wasted have now turned me into some optimist trying to see the possibility in things rather than expecting the worst to be the norm.

I only hope I was able to hold onto it longer than today. I can't imagine going back to the me of a few hours ago, but I suppose it was still an option. Shaking the thought from my mind, I open the door to see my sister standing there and the pizza delivery pulling up on the side of the road. What perfect timing, and just another thing to add to the list of what has gone right for me today.

My sister walked in and turned to stare at me while I tipped the pizza guy. As I shut the door and looked over at her, the confused look on her face stopped me in mid-step.

"What?! Is there something on my face? Oh God that would be just my luc...," and I stop myself. No, that wouldn't be my luck today. That is not the person I am today or what I've come to expect to experience either. I didn't even take the time to check my reflection in the mirror, and my sudden stop was not lost on my sister either.

"No, there's nothing on your face, but there is definitely something different about you. What did you do?"

It wasn't a question; she wasn't asking if I had gone to get my haircut or if I was wearing a new shirt or something. It was an accusation. She sensed something different about me, and she couldn't manage to put her finger on it, so obviously, I had done something wrong.

"I'm just in a good mood today, is all. Don't question it, just let me go with it, alright?"

I wasn't ready to reveal my change in status on the wheel of fortune just yet, and the pizza was here, and I was starving. I set us up at the table, and we fell into those familiar roles talking about the mundane trappings of the day. I could tell she wanted to say more, but something was holding her back from sharing. I had my own secret, but there was something wrong behind her eyes, and I needed her to spit it out. I didn't want to go off on some adventure of fantastic news in front of her if she was struggling. I knew if I did, she'd never tell me what was wrong.

After a bit of poking and prodding, she finally broke down and sat on the edge of tears. The reason she needed to see me today wasn't just for shits and giggles. She had been crying and hurting from what she had found when she returned home from work yesterday. She hadn't told a soul and wasn't sure how to process any of it to begin with either. She had been living with this man that none of us liked mind you for about three or four months now. He hadn't even pulled the boxes he'd brought over out of the garage yet to unpack them, but how do you tell someone without them becoming defensive that you didn't think he was as committed as she might have thought if over half of his clothes were still packed up in boxes? The answer is, you don't. That's one of those lessons you have to learn on your own, and today she was feeling that lesson more completely than she wanted to be.

As she cried, I held her close and let her know that there were still two brothers to tell, and I was pretty sure that they would be on their way to look for the missing roommate to impart a few words of, let's say, understanding on her behalf. She fought the idea and begged me not to tell them. She was embarrassed enough that he left, but she had yet to tell me the worst part. This man child didn't just go with his things, but he had managed to wipe out her entire account in the process. I bet none of you can guess at the amount she was now missing of her own hard-earned money she had been saving. Not entirely what I had unearthed from some random scratch-off ticket, but pretty damn close. Dammit! Somehow, I knew it wasn't really mine, but I meant what I said earlier, the money could disappear. I knew there was something different about my circumstances and having some money I didn't wake up with not be there when I went to bed, didn't seem to matter one bit. I had something else now; I had found something that I could only equate to faith-somehow knowing that it was all going to be alright and that I would be more than okay.

I couldn't promise that I wouldn't share the situation with our brothers, that's just not how it works, and she knew it. However, I promised that she didn't need to worry about the money he took and that she hadn't lost a thing. I sat her back down and explained the events of my day and how she could have every penny, and in fact, I wrote her a check right then to start her a new account in the morning. I wanted to be sure he wouldn't accidentally find his way back into her old account to find a fresh nest egg waiting and him hungry for an omelet.

The shock on her face wasn't from my generosity, not that she wasn't grateful for it, but from the fact that I had won anything. She and I both were flabbergasted at the idea, and I went on to explain just how careful I had been as I transported the winning ticket throughout the day to find its eventual holding area until I could give it to her. She didn't laugh, only nodded along in agreement that I had made the same decisions she would have had it been her. I think she even piped in for a second scared I was going to pull up into the drive-thru at the bank.

"What if it had flown out of your hand?"

She gasped at the idea, and we laughed at the fact that I had that same fear and couldn't allow myself the convenience and walked inside to make my deposit. She did giggle for too long when I told her I wouldn't leave the bank without checking the balance in my account first. She was as amazed and speechless as I had been at what all had transpired. I even told her how I had almost managed to miss the turn onto my street because I had hit every green light on the way home while jamming to my favorite song on the radio. She just shook her head in disbelief and picked up a piece of pizza to chew the whole story over.

After a while of talking in circles about my change of luck, I told her that it wasn't my luck, but it had ended up being hers as well. Had I not been caught off guard and decided to be sensible and walked out of the store without that clover-covered teaser, I wouldn't have been able to gift her what she had lost and needed. I was grateful to be the middleman on this mission; I just wished she didn't have to deal with the pain attached to it all. She smiled and hugged me tighter than I think she ever had before. It was getting late and time for her to head home, and I needed some sleep myself. We hugged again, and I found my way to bed.

With the morning came a sense of peace I had never awaken to before. I had worried that it would wear off once I closed my eyes, and my life would push that restart switch and stick me right back to where I was the day before I had experienced that bit of luck. It hadn't, and I felt just as amazing this morning as I had when I laid down. This was a new sensation, and I wasn't sure how to act, so I just went about business as usual.

It was the weekend, and I had no plans. This was going to be a relaxing day at home, and I couldn't wait. That was the plan until my phone buzzed on the table. Looking down, my brother apparently was going to decide I had other things to do. We discussed what had happened to our sister and how she had called him late last night to tell him about my luck-filled day. After a bit, the reason he called so early on a Saturday became clear. My truck and I were needed because his television went out, and here he was, ready to upgrade to one that wasn't about to fit across his backseat. He at least threw in the promise of lunch when it was all said and done, but honestly, it sounded a lot more fun than sitting around the house all day staring at a wall.

Heading over to pick him up, we spent the drive talking about his family and how they were all doing. Well, that and how excited he was about this giant tv his wife had agreed to let him bring home. Of course, negotiations were involved, and several "honey-do" jobs were waiting for him over the next few weeks in return. He didn't care, he was yammering on about how the football players were going to be life-sized on Sunday when he sat on the couch to watch the game, and that was all that mattered to him.

We pulled up to the store, and I almost stayed in the truck, he didn't need me to pay for any television, and well, I'd given all of that away to our sister just the night before. For some reason, I changed my mind at the last minute and decided to follow him inside. I'm not even sure he knew I was behind him, but as I stepped through the door, the sounds and things flying at my face made me scream in fear. He turned to see me covered in confetti and a handful of employees blowing on little hand-held horns at my face jumping up and down in excitement.

He started laughing as I was ducking and covering, thinking I was under attack. What the hell was going on here? You'd thought I'd won the store, and once the confetti finally settled and the rest of the people around had stopped staring at me, it was explained that I had won. What that was exactly, I was yet to know, but the look on my brother's face as his jaw bounced off the floor at me winning anything for the second time in two days was worth the loss in hearing, I had surely earned just moments ago.

Some woman in a store shirt began to manhandle me a bit and turned me this way and that way for pictures, all while detailing some mess about the store's anniversary giveaway or something and explaining how my now lucky ass had won the grand prize to celebrate. Did anyone even know they were doing this? Apparently not, because marketing has not been key in the overwhelming success of this mom and pop over the years.

My face, still covered in a look of confusion that will no doubt be memorialized in the dozens of photos being taken, just stared ahead, trying to piece together all the words she was shouting in my ear. There was definitely going to be hearing loss attributed to this one, and I'm not sure anymore if I'm going to toss this one under my new "luck" list or not.

As she keeps pointing in the direction of the cameras telling me to smile, a couple of employees come rolling up with a massive box on some platform, and I watched as my brother's eyes lit up like a kid on Christmas morning. Not only had I won, but I'd won a bigger television than he had planned on buying. Some monstrosity that wasn't about to fit along any wall in my house, but I bet if I asked my brother, he'd have just the perfect place for it. I couldn't stop laughing. In two days, I had managed to win exactly what two of my siblings either needed or wanted, and honestly, I couldn't be happier. Just like yesterday, I hadn't woke up with this tv this morning. I sure as hell wasn't going to miss it when I went to bed later tonight, either.

I nodded to my brother, and he started jumping around like a crazy man. I'm willing to bet he's going to try and wiggle his way out of that list of chores after not having actually bought a television too. I know his wife, and good luck with that one. She'll have him over at my house, resodding the lawn on top of all the things she has planned for him. Maybe I did win something after all.

They get this giant box loaded into the back of my truck, and I was practically giggling all the way to his house to drop it off. You'd have thought he'd won some championship all on his own he was so excited, and seeing it slapped across his face just made me happier.

He started laughing so hard at one point I thought he was going to choke to death, and I had to ask what was so funny now? He began to tell me that our brother's business had been operating the last year at a loss and that if he didn't come up with about $250,000, he would have to sell it or shut it down.

"If you're not careful, he's going to be dragging you around to every store he can find to see if some lotto ticket speaks to you for him or not."

Laughing at the idea and the absurdity, I went on to explain the only way I was ever going to be able to come up with that kind of money was to die. He's going to have to come up with something else if he wants to cash in on this lucky streak I'm having because I'm pretty sure those scratch-offs don't pay that well for anyone. We both can't stop laughing at the idea, and he tries to determine if there are enough stores in town for me to get lucky once at each of them to build up to the needed salvation amount. The thought of spending days in and out of convenience stores does not in any way sound convenient or fun, and it definitely doesn't sound lucky.

I push the thought aside as we pull into his driveway, and I remember we now have to figure out how to unload this thing. Lucky for us, my other brother pulls in behind us, and the two of them sound like the older men they are carrying it inside. That entertainment made all of the other mess worth it.

My sister-in-law and I spend the rest of the afternoon watching the two of them refuse to read a single direction as they hung it onto its new home on the wall and laughed at them even more as they tried to figure out how to program it. With that still to tackle, it was time for me to head home. All of us still a little shocked by recent events, and my other brother was attempting to convince me that it was a good idea to see how many lotto tickets I could win. He even tried to say I could try to make it my new income stream, but I was pretty sure after watching them my whole life, that's not how luck worked.

I couldn't help but think about it all the way home. Trying to find a way to help him somehow; there had to be something I could do. I guess I was so lost in the thought of helping, I never saw a thing, just an overwhelmingly loud sound of something to my left, and as I turned to look, suddenly, there was nothing, absolutely nothing. Well, wasn't that lucky?

Jenny Leidecker

CAGED

ONE

Like an animal, caged and forgotten, pacing back and forth, waiting, nothing to pass the time other than the possibility of sustenance provided a few times a day to mark the hours. I've been a prisoner here for so long, I don't even know what day it is anymore. My mind was tormented by the thoughts within it. My body was strained by the pain pulling in every direction. There's no escape, and I fear that there's no end either.

How do you run away from that which is within? There are things inside that control us, and we can't simply pluck them from ourselves like a dandelion invading the yard. Though, one false move and it spreads like those fluffy white seedlings with one faint breath far and wide. Controlled by something you can't see but that you always feel. Your reserved seat on the teacup ride waiting for you to hop inside. You know, some of it's going to be fun, but then there's that one point where your eyes falter, and the entire world is spinning out of control. Looking up, you find that your companion is some evil thrill-seeker without a care in the world twisting and turning your prison faster and faster on some wild, turbulent path. Your head down, trying to focus, looking up in search of some anchor point only to feel yourself pulled into the whirlwind once more.

Even if you signal the ride operator, they're not concerned with your feeling of fear or your sense of losing control. You paid for your ticket, and this ride isn't over yet. All that's left to do is keep your head down and your eyes closed, ignoring the world around you and cross your fingers in hopes that it will be over soon, or grab hold of the wheel and dive into the turn with it. Snatch the reins with some semblance of authority, owning the choice to be there in the first place, one hand pulling over the other, arms crossing, again and again, turning it harder and faster, until suddenly it's over. You slip into a slow spin, and when it finally comes to a halt, you might be a little shaky for a moment, but your feet are still there underneath you, ready to carry you on to the next ride. There is always the next ride.

Right now, I'm in the middle of the spin, and I can't remember when I got on this ride in the first place. I just remember noticing something odd about the house across the street on a walk a few weeks ago. I'm sure I've walked past it a hundred times before, and I can't recall if it was always there or if this was a new feature adorning the neighborhood. Had that bird not flown in front of me and over that roofline, I may have never noticed it at all. That bird was a warning; it had to have been.

I've never seen anything like it before. I mean, who needs something like that to begin with; I've never known anyone who did. There it was, though, and so damn big. Actually, I should say that there are three of them. Who needs three of them? Much less one that is practically covering the entire footprint of that house. I didn't know people still used them, and why would they with all the other options available nowadays? There has to be a reason for it, and that thought right there is what put me on this ride to begin with, and now I'm quickly spinning out of control.

Sorry, I know I'm sitting here going on and on about it. What do you care about my neighbor's house anyway? Never mind that it has what looks like a giant umbrella skeleton antenna on it. That thing is huge, and just to mess with me, I'm sure, they have two more giant clothesline-style antennae as well. Are they in direct contact with E.T.? Seriously, I've only seen something like that on a broadcasting building or some government agency, not someone's house, and definitely not in the suburbs.

I was speechless. I think I must have stood there for a good ten minutes just staring at it. My eyes squinting in thought, contorting my face into some locked state of confusion. Had someone noticed me there on the side of the road, I would have looked deranged, gawking up at those metal extensions reaching out from that house. My tiny little apartment complex is on the other side of the road, and if I step out onto my balcony, I can see most of this house through the tree that separates us. I've never looked twice at it before, but now, it's all I can think about.

At first, it wasn't so bad. I went home and sat on the couch, a little bewildered at the idea of their existence. I tossed and turned that night, dipping in and out of strange dreams of aliens and surveillance teams huddled at a kitchen table whispering and watching countless monitors all day. Were there cameras on that house too? I've never looked, didn't even cross my mind until now. So many thoughts running through my head as to what was going on behind those walls.

I poured myself a cup of coffee and stepped out onto the balcony. No longer wrapped up in the birds nesting in the tree outside in my courtyard or the sounds of my neighbors heading out for work, nothing else had my attention like that house did now. The sound of my cat chattering away to the nest of blue jays was the only recognition of the outside world beyond the laser beam focus I had on that house. My face twisted in thought, realizing I couldn't remember a single car ever parked in the driveway or anyone pulling in and out of the garage. Two chairs sat empty on the porch, and I can't recall a single instance where anyone was sitting in them. I'd waved or said hello to over half the neighborhood on my daily walks, but there had never been so much as a smile from someone associated with that house. Did anyone even live there?

As I sat staring, the outdoor lights on the porch and near the garage went off, leaving some belief that there had to be an intelligent life form in there with the capability to at least flip a light switch. But, of course, they could have always been on a timer. That could help maintain the look of someone living there, couldn't it? I just didn't know, and my inquisitive nature was quickly turning into an obsession. I moved a small table and my laptop outside facing the house to work that first day. I knew if I could just see one person coming or going or even if they stepped outside to check the mail, I'd be free from the spiraling thoughts that were quickly building into a tornado of crazy inside my head. I was on a mission. I needed to know who lived there and why in the hell they needed that monstrosity on top of their house.

I watched it all day, and not a single curtain fluttered, not one door opened, and even the mail carrier passed by it in such a determined manner, you'd think they had never slid one letter into that mailbox. I suppose it's not too unheard of to stay inside all day, I for one, rarely leave my apartment, other than to venture out for food and such. Maybe this was just one of those days. I can't sit and jump to too many conclusions. It's only been a day that I've taken any time to pay attention to it all. What are my options, though? Do I sit out on my balcony and watch this house every day until someone finally walks out or at least glances out one of the windows? Can you stalk a house?

I really did try to forget about it, but just as I walked back out onto the balcony again, the outside lights flipped back on, and I took note of the time 6:58 pm. That's an odd time, isn't it? Had they had them set up on a timer, you'd suspect they'd come on at the top of the hour, right? Or maybe that's the ploy to making it look natural, that odd time to throw everyone else off. I mean, who would think twice about what time their outside lights turned on and off? Still, I jotted it down in my notebook just in case I forgot it the next day. Yeah, it was already decided that there was no way I could walk away from this mystery so soon. I needed answers as to what was going on in that house and who, if anyone, lived there. Just harmless fun, and I can't imagine it's going to take too long to find the answers anyway.

That night I couldn't focus on anything else. I was stuck in a web of thoughts shooting off in some unlikely directions, and each one of them crazier than the last. I poured myself a glass of wine about an hour or so after the lights had flipped on across the street, and there wasn't a single light to be seen on in that house. How is it possible to function in complete darkness? Maybe the windows I can see from this side are bedrooms or bathrooms, and they're in the living room watching television or something. Curiosity grabbed at me and my glass of wine, and I slipped down the stairs and over to the edge of my little complex to catch a glimpse of the front of this house. I could see what looked like one tiny lamp glowing through one of the curtains, no flicker from a television screen, none of the main lights on in the house, just one little lamp. I suppose it is past dinner time, and it is possible they could be in there enjoying a good book. Obviously, people still read. It's all just so strange, and before I headed back up to my door, I stared again at those enormous antennas protruding from the roof. My body shivered at the possibilities I had allowed to start forming in my head, and I scurried back up to the safety of my apartment. Once inside, I locked everything up tight and crawled into bed with my own book in an attempt to push the intrusive thoughts from my mind long enough to find some sleep. Whether or not that would happen was still yet to be seen.

CAGED

TWO

I tossed and turned all night. Between nightmares and fog-filled thoughts in those moments between sleep, I'm not sure I managed more than a couple of hours of rest all put together. When I finally fell out of bed, I was more tired than I had been when I crawled into it hours before. Today was going to be a coffee-fueled day, and I'm not sure the pot was ever going to be empty.

I grabbed a cup and a muffin from the counter and nearly rushed outside to see if maybe someone was up moving around this morning. If the thought of this house was going to keep me up more than half the night, I would need to get some answers sooner rather than later. Lack of sleep is never good for anyone, and I am beyond horrible once I get too tired. Sure, one night of restless sleep, but much more than that, and I forget how to function like a normal human being.

Standing there at the edge of the balcony, I again block out the beauty of the morning around me and immediately focus on that house half-hidden by that tree. That damn tree. I swear, if I had a chainsaw, I'd trim a few branches out of my way this morning. I'm sure it's the reason I missed any possible movement from anyone inside of there. I can barely see the front door as it is, and what if they did pop their head out for some reason, and I missed it because of that stupid tree. Taking another sip of coffee, I realized I hadn't even taken my walk yesterday for fear of missing any happenings going on there. I would have to remember to take the break and at least have a short walk around the block. I still needed to look to see if there were any cameras set up around that property. I can't believe I forgot to notice yesterday when I ran down there with my wine. Security cameras would just add to the list of conspiracies piling up in my head all over a couple of antennas attached to their roof. Let's be honest, those were not just your average garden variety options, and I was no closer to figuring out what they might be for than I was two days ago when I first noticed them.

With the end of that thought and what was undoubtedly a hundred more, the outside lights flipped off again. I hadn't noticed yesterday just what time it was, but I took a quick note that it was 7:12 a.m. and quickly wrote it down in my notebook next to the time from last night. Another odd time to think it might be on a timer. Surely someone is in there sipping on their own coffee and just happened past the switch and turned it off before forgetting and leaving it on all day. I can't imagine how many times I would forget to turn them off if I spent all day inside not seeing them and kicking myself for wasting filament later.

My cat spent the morning in blissful splendor, and I stared nonstop at every detail I could memorize of this house. I waited for one of the lights in any of the windows to turn on but not one ever did while I sat finishing my coffee. Reluctantly I jumped in the shower and washed as quickly as humanly possible, nearly slipping and busting my head open once in the process. Then, pulling my hair back, tossing on some clothes, and grabbing my laptop, I made my way back out onto the balcony and set up for the day. I honestly don't think I made much headway in the work I needed to do yesterday, and today was quickly turning into a repeat of that same amount of progress. I couldn't tear my eyes away long enough to read an entire email in one glance. Around lunchtime, I finally gave up on trying to accomplish anything, closed my computer, and headed out for a walk. I needed a break from it all, but most of all, I needed to see if I could detect any movement inside that house so I could finally stop obsessing about it and get back to my real life.

I rounded the block three times, each time slowing down considerably to try and peek through the windows and glance around the perimeter for any cameras or anything unusual for that matter. There was nothing, absolutely nothing. I couldn't tell, but it appeared that same little lamp was still on towards the back of the house, but there was nothing else. How is all of this possible? What if I just walked up to the front door and knocked on it to just introduce myself? The thought alone spiked a level of anxiety I didn't know existed within me. It felt like the equivalent of purposefully typing something into your search box that you knew would set off alarms with the FBI and add your now eclectic search history into some file in their database with your name on it. I wasn't nearly brave enough for either of those options, and I made my way back to my apartment and up the stairs.

I hadn't been gone but maybe an hour, but something felt different walking into my personal space. It was like I knew this mystery wasn't going to end as quickly and as easily as I had hoped, but also, I could feel that it was almost as if the house had moved part of itself into my space. That sounds weird, I know, and I can't explain it any better than that. Something had changed. Even my cat was acting strange when I walked in from my walk. He would typically greet me at the door but instead ran and hid under my bed for a moment before realizing it was me and coming out again. He'd never been scared of anything before, and it shook me. I'm sure it's all in my head and shaking it off, I head back outside to continue my watch party of this house that hasn't done anything but exist for the last few days, and well, you'd think that would be enough, but I needed movement. I need to find some understanding as to what is happening over there.

CAGED

THREE

My life was quickly starting to exist on that balcony. I barely allowed myself any time inside at all, other than to prepare a little something to eat, attempt to sleep, and use the facilities when necessary. I nearly forgot to stop watching the house long enough to eat dinner, and just to be sure I didn't wither away to nothing while clearly obsessing over all of this, I set up a few alarms on my phone to remind me to eat. Surely this would all be over tomorrow, though. I mean, how many days can someone stay inside without ever leaving? I was hoping the answer to that was only two and that tomorrow, on the third day, there would be some movement. Better yet, maybe they'd at least look out the window at some point tonight. That would definitely make for a better night's sleep for me. I suppose it wouldn't answer all of my questions, but it would at least give me some relief that a real person lived inside of there.

Looking down again at my notebook to confirm

the time and once more at my phone, I barely blinked as the last few seconds of time disappeared forever. Staring into the darkness of the light bulbs themselves to ensure I didn't miss the moment they turned on, and just like clockwork, 6:58 began, and the outside lights on the house blinked into existence once more. I couldn't help but smile and giggle even at the realization that surely it wasn't possible for someone inside that house to pick the exact same time to turn the outside lights on two nights in a row. It really isn't possible, is it? They had to be on a timer, which only adds to my suspicion that no one actually lives there.

Bouncing into the house, I pour myself a glass of wine in almost a celebratory manner, as if I had just discovered the world was round, and I couldn't wait to share it with everyone else. Unfortunately, once that first sip hit my lips, I was back in the storm again. What if they're just on vacation and they purposefully set a timer on their lights for while they were gone? It would explain everything up to this point, even the mail. They could have put a hold on everything while they're gone and who knows how long that might be. Dammit! I could be watching a house that's empty for recreational purposes. I can't spend a week or more watching this house until the possibility of someone finally coming home. I'll go mad.

With determination, I grabbed my glass of wine and again started my way down the stairs, this time grabbing a bag of trash that needed to go out to keep from looking like a crazy person in the middle of the parking lot staring at someone's house. From the dumpster, I could tell that the same little lamp was on in the back of the house and nothing else. It makes too much sense now that they're just away on vacation or something. However, the weekend starts tomorrow, and if they are, they'll likely be back in just a couple of days. So I could give it a bit of a rest until then, and I'm sure my pillow would also appreciate the usage.

I get myself back inside and clear my things off the balcony, and go to take one last look at that house before giving up for the night. Everything was quiet and the same as it all had been, except for one slight difference, the garage door was more than halfway closed and still closing. Nearly falling over the edge of the balcony, I tried desperately to determine if there was a car parked inside or if the garage light was even on, but it all happened so fast, and the door was closed before I could see anything at all. So what the hell was that? Is someone home now? Were they always there, and they just live in dim light or something? What is going on right now?

I tried to recreate my walk from the trash to pick out any sounds or movements I might have seen surrounding that house, but there was nothing. I had become so resound with the fact that they had to be away on vacation that I completely ignored it after that. I was elated at the idea of it all that the house ceased to exist in reality for the entire walk back. I can't believe it. How did I miss it? I have been so hyper-focused on that corner that I could barely see straight anymore, and here I went and missed the one clue I could have had as to who was living inside of it. I'm never going to sleep now. Damn that house!

CAGED

FOUR

I couldn't stop staring at it all over again. As if it had been that long, to begin with, but still, I was back to square one. No other lights came on while I sat there and finished my wine, and I couldn't find a single piece of trash to require me to walk back down to the dumpster again either. There was no way I was about to go down there and just stare at it now. The idea of it gave me just as much anxiety as the thought to go and knock on the door had before. I'm not sure I even remembered how to blink for a bit there, if I'm honest. Looking down at the time and my empty glass, I knew I needed to climb into bed and try to sleep, as foreign as that concept seemed to be right now. But, I at least had to try. There was one more day of work I needed to attempt to participate in somehow, and then surely this mystery would be over. Especially now that there had been some kind of movement there. They can't avoid me forever, can they?

Whether it was the exhaustion from two nights

of very little sleep or the added knowledge that there was someone in there or, for that matter, that there had at least been someone in there that allowed me to fall deep into sleep, but I needed it badly. I dreamt of walking around the block at least a dozen times, and not once had anything changed. I was determined to exhaust myself one way or another, it seemed. The added exercise must have been what stirred my body. My brain had had enough walking around for one night, and surely that's what had forced me to start waking in the first place. Although, in the background, I could hear voices, and maybe I had left the TV on, but I don't remember turning it on, only falling through the mattress into a walking dream. Seriously, I better have lost a few pounds after that one. I'm sure that's wishful thinking, though.

The room was completely dark, and both televisions were silent. I know there was talking. I heard it at that moment between waking and my dreams. I didn't imagine it. Lying still, my ears perked up like a dog that just heard a can opener start a mile away. Trying not to open my eyes too much, I needed to focus on the sounds around me, and before I could think on it too much, there it was again. The static of a radio signal just out of tune and barely audible before one sentence broke in through the silence, and I flew out of bed looking for its source. One sentence.

"She's awake."

I heard it. I know I did, and it was right here in my room. I grabbed at the alarm clock, ensuring the radio hadn't accidentally turned on, and my phone to see if some new alert had popped up. Surely in my half-asleep brain, I had misheard it, and it was something else altogether. Nothing. I grabbed at the remote and smashed the power button. Maybe there was something wrong with my screen, but the volume was still working somehow. As I released the button, the welcome screen illuminated there in front of me, and I choked back a scream. Nothing else inside my apartment could have made any noise that I might mistake for any voice talking, much less one announcing that I'm awake.

What the hell was happening here? Just as the thought entered my mind, along with the panic, I heard my neighbor bang into the wall, and I finally started breathing again. I hadn't realized I wasn't breathing, to begin with, as I sat there in silence, sniffing out the source of what had just freaked me the hell out. It had to have been the neighbors. It was the only explanation that made any sense. I needed it to have been them. All the other possibilities were beyond frightening. Honestly, I'm not sure what any of those possibilities might be anyway.

Catching a glimpse at the clock, it was only three. No wonder it was still so dark out. I took another breath and headed to the kitchen, hoping a glass of water and a few steps might clear my head enough to let me get back to sleep again. Grabbing a glass and some water from the tap, I can't concentrate on anything but how clear and close those words had sounded. Maybe some fresh air will help clear my mind a little, and as I stepped out onto the balcony, the glass almost slipped from my hand onto the concrete under my feet. Every light in that house was on. The entire thing was lit up like darkness wasn't allowed to exist within those walls.

This isn't real. Surely I'm still dreaming. Why in the world would every light be on at this hour? Every window may be lit up, but I can't see anyone moving inside. Nothing, there is absolutely nothing I can see inside of that house. The curtains are just thick enough. I can't make out what might be furniture or what could be an actual person from here, and I sure as hell am not about to walk down there in the middle of the night either. I don't care how curious I am. It just seems like that might turn into some disappearance I don't want to be a part of since I'd likely be the one disappearing.

As if my thoughts and curiosity somehow permeated the walls all of a sudden. I swore I heard the same voice that had awaken me moments earlier.

"Turn them off," and before I could flip around to see where that voice was coming from, every light turned off at the same time. Again the entire house was shrouded in darkness. This time my glass wasn't as lucky, and it slipped through my fingers, shattering into a thousand pieces at my feet.

It doesn't make any sense, and I couldn't move for a moment as the reality of what just happened seeped its way into my brain. I rubbed my eyes and leaned forward over the balcony, careful not to move my feet for fear of the cuts all that glass would create, but this couldn't be real, could it? I'm losing my mind, or I'm still asleep, and this is all part of some weird dream pulling me further down the rabbit hole. That had to be it. This was not happening.

It was the only reality I could believe right now, and I turned to walk inside, careful to avoid the glass that surely wasn't there, and walked back to bed. Crawling between the sheets, I let myself fall back into sleep so quickly because I had to have been asleep already. I had to be.

CAGED

FIVE

Waking the next morning, I laid there listening. I needed to be sure there was no voice this time and accept what happened last night for the dream it had to have been. So I waited a full five minutes, tossing and turning, barely opening my eyes and making all of those "I'm waking up" sounds to see if I could provoke the voice to return, but there was nothing, just as I had hoped or expected since it all had undoubtedly been a dream.

Finally tossing the covers off of me, I stumbled in to brush my teeth and work my way through my morning routine, still trying to shake off the dream I had last night. This house was really starting to get to me. Nothing had ever taken over so many of my thoughts like this before.

It wasn't until I walked into the living room that I knew it had all been real, or at least I had been up and experienced something. The balcony door was still slightly open, and the shards of glass covered the concrete. Unable to move for a moment, I played out the night's events again and yet still couldn't believe any of it had happened, but the evidence was right there. I had no doubt something had woken me from my dreams, and to admit I had heard someone's voice breaking through the silence of my room was too much to take in right now. How could I have heard it? Where could it be coming from? How could anyone have brought anything in here to spy on me like that? No one had been here, and the only times I had ever left my apartment were for my walks. Could that be it? Could they, whoever "they" are, have broken into my apartment while I was out and added surveillance? That's silly, and the thought just makes me feel more than a bit ridiculous and paranoid. I hadn't done anything to draw that kind of attention to myself, and god knows I'm not important enough to be spied on in the first place.

Shaking my head for the umpteenth time since his house grabbed my attention, I forced myself to believe that my lack of sleep and crazy thought of what could possibly be, you know, like if somehow my life was now a horror novel, was driving these ridiculous experiences. It was all in my head. It had to be all in my head. The alternative was too scary to believe anymore.

I pushed myself forward, forcing myself to start my morning routine. I set up the coffee pot and let it begin to brew, but instead of sitting there staring at it and willing it to work faster, I grabbed my broom and dustpan to take on the mess from the night before. I kept my head down the entire time, refusing to look over at the house, just sitting there taunting me. Attempting to push the hold of every fear I now had away, refusing to give it control over my day. Out of sight, out of mind, right?

I managed to avoid it for the few minutes I was out there, but grabbing my cup of coffee, I noticed the clock sat there with only two minutes before the outside lights went off yesterday. Here was my moment, was I going to sit out there again all day watching this house, or was I going to let it go and ignore whatever possibilities may be attached to it?

Taking that first sip and noticing the cat already hanging out on the ledge watching the birds in the tree taunting him, I knew I was now the same as him. Hypnotized by the comings and goings of a house that wasn't about to give me answers any more than those birds were going to fly over into the reach of my waiting cat. Wishful thinking on both our parts, I think, and with a sigh, I stepped out just in time to see the lights turn off right at 7:12 am. It was going to be another long day.

CAGED

SIX

I sat out on the balcony again for the entire day, barely focusing on anything other than that house. Not a minute of work getting done. If I wasn't trying to figure out a way to see through the brick, I was staring off into space, reliving the events of the night before. That voice replaying in the back of my mind, and each time creating more uneasiness than the last. It all had to be something else. It had to have been the neighbors, and seeing all of the lights on last night, that had to be a twisted trick of the mind trying to make this all something it isn't. I can't believe the alternative, not yet, and I'm not sure I ever wanted to either.

Sitting there staring, I almost zoned in and out of sleep a few times. No real rest for the last two nights was finally starting to catch up with me. It was in one of those moments of drifting off that I heard that sound again. The static of an untuned radio echoing through my apartment and reaching me outside. Not wanting to make any sudden moves in fear of it disappearing again, I sat pretending like I didn't hear a thing, all the while trying to convince myself that I actually wasn't hearing anything. But I was, the white noise almost getting louder the more I tried to ignore it, or I was only focusing harder on the sound bringing its existence closer to me in the process. Pecking at my laptop in an attempt to act "normal" for a minute, the voice broke through once more, and with it, there was no mistaking it had come from within my apartment, and it definitely wasn't the neighbors, I had heard them leave an hour ago. But it was as clear as if I was standing right next to them.

"Yes, I can see her."

Not only had the voice solidified the fear I knew I should be feeling, but the words it spoke were terrifying. What did they mean they could see me? Were they even talking about me? Is it because I'm out here on the balcony, and they can see me from the house or are they watching me from inside my own apartment? I had to know. Surely if they had wired anything inside here, I could easily find it, right? I jumped from my chair outside and started on my new mission to find any and all looking and listening devices there might be planted in my space. They had to be in here somewhere. There's nothing else they could be talking about, right? This was not acceptable. They had no right to be watching me like this. What had I ever done to warrant their attention and constant vigil of my life?

Nothing. I was sure of it. Other than some natural curiosity, I hadn't really done anything to that house or anyone who might be inside of it. Hell, I hadn't even taken the time to look up what those things could have been used for in the first place. I just sat there and let the crazy thoughts that had been swirling in my mind the last few days take on a life of their own. I probably should look it up, I'm sure there's a reasonable explanation for it all, and I'm blowing it all out of proportion. First, I'm going to look in every single nook and cranny around here to make sure there isn't a single camera watching me, and if I can figure out where that voice is coming from, too, that would be fantastic. I'd really like to sleep tonight and now is my opportunity to help quiet some of those fears by making sure there is nothing inside my own personal space connected to that house or, honestly, anything that could be keeping an eye on me. I'm in search of their little devices and a little bit of peace in the process.

Tearing the apartment apart, I look on every bookshelf, behind everything that could or couldn't move. II even examined the light switches and electrical outlets, I couldn't find anything, but there had to be something. How else could they see me and I hear them if there wasn't? It doesn't make any sense, and I know I heard it. That wasn't the middle of the night, and yes, I might have been tired, but I was still awake, at least for the most part anyway. Maybe that's it. Maybe my mind is starting to create all of this on its own now that I'm so tired. I haven't slept more than a few hours the last couple of nights, and the lack of sleep is definitely starting to wear on my body as well. I feel like I'm dragging a truck behind me with each step, and as I look at the clock inching closer to seven, I grab a glass of wine and go stand in anticipation of those outside lights to turn back on again. Right on schedule, they flip on and illuminate a house that I still have no clue whether anyone is actually in there or not.

I couldn't do this again. I needed sleep. Finishing up my glass of wine, I drop it into the sink, lock up the doors, and head to bed. My eyelids already attempting to take me hostage for the next several hours with each step I get closer to my pillow. Crawling into what will surely be a coma, I feel myself drift off into a dream before I can even consider that house one more time today. Of course, as soon as the fog lifted, I was standing there in front of it all over again, trying to move closer towards the windows in order to get a look inside. If I'm lucky, I'll find a few answers looking in there, but as I start to walk up to the glass, I could just barely hear something. Some kind of crackling, and as I turn to look for the source, I find myself instead staring up at my ceiling in the dark. The now-familiar sound breaking through my dream and echoing off of my bedroom walls. Turning my head to look over at the clock, midnight was staring back at me brightly, and I was done. Yelling into the void that was my room, I expected answers.

"What the hell do you want?"

The only response was the one I had heard before, stiff and matter of fact.

"She's awake."

CAGED

SEVEN

They were the only words spoken again. The static returning once more and then the silence. I flung the blankets off me, more angry at being awake than the intrusion of that voice this time. I'm past exhausted, and the lack of sleep was pushing me far past a little upset or inconvenienced. Walking into the bathroom, I couldn't stop myself from ranting at this invisible watcher I now apparently was sharing space with for some reason.

"Well, what do you want? Are you just going to sit there and watch me all the time? Are you enjoying watching me while I go to the bathroom? Perverts!"

Washing my hands and splashing a little water on my face that was already a bit red from getting frustrated, I asked again.

"I asked you a question. What do you want?"

Nothing. It was as if they shut everything off once I woke up again. Well, I can't be bothered with this anymore, and I'm not going to let some strange voice who isn't willing to engage me when I talk to it ruin any more of my sleep. I plopped myself into bed and settled back in, ready to fall asleep and ignore the voice, at least for tonight. Almost drifting again into my dream world, the static noise returned. I peeked over at the clock with half an eye open, and I hadn't been back between the covers for more than thirty minutes or so. Sitting up, I nearly growl at the sound. Searching the darkness for some kind of light or anything that might indicate where that noise was coming from, but there was nothing. Words just about to form on my lips to question whatever this was again, and then, silence.

Sighing, I fell back into my pillow and tried to cover my ears as best I could just in case the sound returned. I needed sleep, and allowing them to torture me was not on my list of things to do tonight. If I could just get another five or six hours of uninterrupted sleep, I would almost be myself again. I could then look at this all a little more level-headed and rationally. All I really need is some sleep. Please, just let me sleep again.

I breathed out the thought and tried hard not to let the ideas of it all take over, and settling back into my pillow, I fell back to sleep once more. I had just started dreaming, something about a dog that was meowing because the entire world is upside down right now when I could hear the static once again. Pulling me from any type of rest, I groaned once more, lifting my head to look over at the clock. At least it had been a little more than an hour this time, they must be taking pity on me and my exhaustion or they're letting me only get right to sleep in a sick and twisted game of torturing me. Hanging my head in what was most assuredly going to be my defeat, in the end, I nearly cried at how desperately I wanted to be left alone. How much I just wanted to be allowed to sleep while it was dark outside. This does not seem like an unrealistic request, but I knew at that moment that was not something I was going to get tonight.

"You win."

It was all I could manage in what was barely a whisper, and I wasn't even sure anyone else heard me. I was too tired to fight anymore, and I dropped my head back onto my pillow and pulled the second one on top of me to shield my ears from what I knew would be another invasion of sound soon enough. I would have to grab at every minute of sleep I could to keep my sanity. That's something I'm not sure I have a tight enough grip on right now, either. It'll have to be the first question I tackle once the sun comes up, though. One, I hope I don't feel the need to contemplate over long.

CAGED

EIGHT

All night I fought the sounds of static and that voice announcing on occasion that I was yet again awake, just to remind me that not only could I hear them, but that they could see me as well. I hadn't earned enough sleep to even piece together a single dream from all the fragments I was awarded when my eyes closed, and as the sun started to peek through the curtains, I finally gave up on trying.

It's the weekend, and I should be enjoying sleeping in as much as I'd like, but sleep has been elusive for days now. I can feel the weight of the bags under my eyes with every step and blink I take. Staring at the coffee pot and willing it to finish faster, the call from outside was practically screaming my name. Maybe if I sat outside on the balcony, I might be able to sneak a nap far away from the sounds of that voice, and whoever it was that felt the need to start torturing me like this. Completely useless is what I am, and there's no getting away with trying to function anywhere other than here until I can find some actual sleep.

I've become a prisoner in my own home with exhaustion standing guard as my warden. Dead on my feet and on the edge of crazy is where I feel like I am. Barely able to complete one thought, much less attempt to determine what it is that I'm truly dealing with here. What is this game I've been tossed into? Curiosity killed the cat, and I'm starting to feel a lot like my feline roommate at this point. I can't make it through another night without any real sleep, I can't. I need to find the source of that noise and where that voice is coming from.

That's it. That has to be the plan. I have to find where it is they can see me, and where it is they're broadcasting into my room. It's real. I know it, and somehow they've found a way to plant a camera and speaker in my apartment. Even though I couldn't find it the other day, it's here somewhere, it has to be, but where?

Taking another sip of coffee, attempting to clean the cobwebs out of my mind, I took another hard look at the house that has started to control my life, all while cemented to that plot of land. Trying to will some form of x-ray vision into existence, my new nemesis reached out through the void once more. That now all to familiar sound of static making its way to me out on the balcony, and that was it. I couldn't take it any longer, and another cup lost its life to the concrete beneath my feet. Leaping to my new mission, I stepped into the living room, listening with every ounce of my being in search of a direction from which the sound was coming from.

It's impossible! I thought for sure it was going to have to come from a shared wall with one of my neighbors. There's no other way they could have done it, but there was no doubt, the static was clearly coming from the wall separating my living room and bedroom. How is that possible? There's no way anyone could have planted some kind of speaker in that wall. I've only been out of here at most an hour at a time. How could they have done something like that in such a short amount of time? The other question I still needed answered was, why me? Nothing I've done has given reason to place me under surveillance, and for a split second, I again questioned my sanity. Then, as if they could see my disbelief written across my face, the voice cut through the static once more.

"She can see us."

I locked my eyes to the spot on the wall but could see nothing but sheetrock there. I couldn't see anything out of place. Determination driving each step closer to that spot, I could just barely make out a small round patch that I can't ever remember being there before. They were right, I could see it now, and there was no unseeing it. Finally, a way to stop the sound, to kill the noise and that voice. There was going to be a celebratory nap after I destroyed that speaker. I don't care if they can see me anymore, I'd found their speaker, and it was only a matter of time before I found the camera as well.

Walking over to the drawer in the kitchen, I knew exactly what I needed to remedy this problem. I'd fix the wall later, but the first thing on my list after hammering that speaker into dust was going to be sleep. Raring back, I smashed the head of the hammer through the wall right at that little patched circle, hoping to do damage to that damn speaker in the process, but as I pulled it from the newly created hole, there was nothing there but the backside of my bedroom wall. Opening up the flashlight on my phone and illuminating what bits I could see, it was empty. Maybe I hit the wrong spot, but the rest of the wall was perfect, and my aim had hit its mark dead on. Slipping my finger in, searching for any wires or anything at all, and still nothing.

"She's searching."

I could hear the echo up through the hole. I know it's in there, and well, the damage is already done. Why stop now? Taking another swing, I slam through once more, but it still isn't big enough for my hand to reach through, and that's the new goal. Over and over and over again, I breach the surface. Finally, I'm able to reach inside and end this madness. Breaking off a few more pieces to ensure I wouldn't scratch myself, I slip my hand inside blindly, searching for my tormentor, not once considering the dangers of the wiring throughout that I would surely come in contact with at some point. Oh well, maybe it would shock me just enough to knock me out for a few hours. I'm willing to take the sleep where I can get it now.

Nothing. Nothing but a hollow wall, and again the static breaks the silence. I could hear it clearly coming from the cavity I'd created in my wall. I may need to hire someone to repair this when I'm done, but I couldn't care less. Using the pry bar on the hammer, I start ripping away chunks of the wall down to the floor. Once I peel back the last piece of sheetrock, the static stops, and I find no speaker, only a six-inch-wide section of my wall missing and a giant mess on the floor.

Now I was just angry and practically delirious. Grabbing at the wall, I ripped off a huge chunk and kept going. The whole thing was going to need to be replaced anyway. I might as well clear it out of the way and find that damn speaker. I had to find it, and I knew it was somewhere in this wall. Then, as if trying to be some voice of reason, the static broke through again, and the voice demanded at once.

"Stop!"

Hearing it only drove me harder. I was close. I had to be. Why else would they want me to stop? I was onto their little game now, and furiously I ripped away every piece of covering from the studs with my bare hands. Stepping back, I can feel the smile burst across my face as if I had accomplished some amazing feat. I was proud that I had torn it all down, but as I stepped closer, breathing heavily, I looked down to find absolutely nothing. I couldn't take it anymore and crumbled into a puddle on the floor to cry. I had been so sure it would be there. It had to be there, or else I'm just some crazy person that ripped down an entire wall for nothing. I am not crazy. I'm just tired, and I'm not myself when I don't get enough sleep. That's all this is.

My sudden burst of energy drained me, and I needed to rest. Halfway crawling into my room, I climb back into bed, too tired to care where they are hidden any longer. Closing my eyes, I toss a quick thought out into the universe, begging for a bit of silence, just long enough for me to sleep.

Thirty minutes, that's as long as they allowed me, but it felt like a luxury. That tiny nap was just enough to give me some clarity and energy. The static breaking through my dreams is the alarm I've become accustomed to these last couple of days, to the point it wasn't even shocking anymore, just some white noise that would pull me from my slumber all too quickly. I opened my eyes to the random announcement that barely rattled me anymore.

"She's awake."

My own personal narration of my life and the static creating the soundtrack. Time no longer mattered, and I ripped the cord to my alarm clock from the wall to stop the numbers shining back at me and from taunting me. Throwing it into the wall that separated my room from the bathroom, it left its own hole in the sheetrock before falling to the ground. That was it, the only solution I could think of now, and I sprung to my feet with a newfound plan pulling the pictures from the wall. I knew it was the only way now. I'm going to tear down every single wall until I find them until I destroy them and claim my life back as my own and not whatever it was in that house.

That house just sitting over there in silence, in the dark, watching me. Keeping me awake like an experiment in sleep deprivation. I'm not going to let them win. I can't. I'm going to find all of their little hidden devices and ground them out of existence. They are not going to win, and they will never break me. They'd never have the chance now. I'm going to find every single one and destroy them. Ripping away pieces of the wall from the hole left by what used to be my alarm clock, one thought running through my mind over and over again until, at some point, I realized I was repeating it out loud between giggles.

"I win. I'm going to win. I'm going to beat you."

Once the wall was down, a mess of dust, wires, and chunks of wall scattered everywhere, I looked at my work with a sense of pride. I almost forgot to look for the speaker in the cavity left by my wave of destruction. It didn't matter. There was nothing there. I could hear the static filter in from the living room, and practically possessed with rage, I grabbed the hammer and started in on the next wall as the voice cut through the banging sounds.

"She's gone mad."

Flipping around to face the emptiness of the room, I yelled back into the void.

"I have not! I win. I'm going to win. You will never break me."

Laughing at the ridiculousness of their statement, I again focused on the task at hand. I will find them. I will beat them. I'm not sure how long the banging and pulling and ripping lasted, but looking for a place to sit and stare at my accomplishment proved difficult as everything was covered in debris. There was sheetrock and insulation everywhere and on everything. All that remained was the framing and wires, and I had practically forgotten about what it was I was even searching for until I heard that familiar sound of static radiating from the pile. The voice simply stating.

"We're still here."

That's when I think the madness overcame me. I had been rational up until this point, but they weren't going to win. I wasn't about to let them beat me. This was the moment my teacup ride started spinning out of control, and I couldn't find something to focus on to keep everything from spiraling into oblivion. Whatever was in that house was the ride conductor, and they weren't nearly ready to let me off this one.

CAGED

NINE

I sprung into action and flinging open the balcony door, nearly knocking it off its tracks. I reached down to grab the first piece of the wall lying there in the pile and caught a glimpse of my cat peeking out from his hiding place under the bed. His eyes were wide and nervous as I imagine my redecorating was a slight shock to him, and hiding in the back corner under my bed gave him some cover from the flying debris I had been tossing around without any thought. It would all be over soon enough, and the only thing waking me up with a sense of shock would be him walking across my head at three in the morning. That was something I could handle, but I was over this game derived by some unseen captor. Still, in search of that speaker, I slowly and thoroughly examined every piece of wall and insulation I picked out of the pile before tossing it out over the balcony. Checking to make sure no one was in my line of sight first, but it was, guessing by the level of light still left in the sky, early evening on Saturday, and I had all day tomorrow to clean up my mess and carry it to the dumpster before anyone truly noticed.

Piece by piece, they flew over the edge, and still, I had found nothing. I could hear a couple of my neighbors talking every now and again, trying to discern what was going on but not concerned enough by it to let it ruin their Saturday night. The pile inside growing smaller, and the walls of my apartment laid broken. Yet, I still hadn't found what I was looking for, and as if on cue, that familiar sound broke through the hollow shell that had once been my dwelling. The static was grating my nerves now, and this game of hide and seek was growing old as they repeated their statement from before. A reminder that they could see me and everything I was doing in my attempts to find them.

"We're still here."

I growled at their taunting and began pulling all of the pieces of my life apart in a craze. Ripping my couch cushions apart, pulling them from their covers, and tossing them over the edge with the rest of the debris. Shaking out books one by one as I flung them to the ground below, no longer caring if anyone was in the cross-hairs, and for the first time, the voice laughed. It was laughing at me. That was it. That was the last straw. Grabbing hold of the hammer, I headed straight for the front door, and as I pushed pieces of wall and a chair out of the way to make my escape, I thought again, maybe I'm taking this all a bit too far. Looking back at the destruction I had created and seeing my unused bed, I was reminded that I'm fine, I'm just tired, and well, I'm not really myself when I'm tired.

The doorway cleared and hammer in hand. I

don't even bother locking the door. Nearly everything I own is on the ground below for anyone to pick through if they wanted. I didn't care about any of that anymore. I knew what I needed to do to free myself from that house. I hadn't hardly looked at it all day while I searched for their little evil devices, but there it stood as if it had nothing to do with keeping me awake these past few days. I don't even know what time it is, and I don't care. I hope they're sleeping in there. It's my turn to wake them up for a change. As I stepped up to the porch, the yard filled with light. Floodlights hitting me from all directions, like one of those thwarted cartoon jailbreak moments that made the escapee freeze. Not me, not this time. They'd have to have a firing squad at the ready to stop me and my mission tonight. I was going to make them tell me exactly where they had hidden those cameras and speakers if it were the last thing I did.

Reaching the door, any levels of anxiety I had experienced before at this thought were long gone, and my need for answers now took control. I knocked first like a normal person would. I'm not crazy after all. After three breaths, I counted, and there was no movement inside at all, so I rang the bell. Obviously, it was the next reasonable action in these situations. Still nothing, that was it, I had played their game long enough, and I was going to tear down the door if I had to in order to get to them inside of there.

Hammer in hand, I swing it as hard as possible, but it didn't push through the surface as I had hoped, but of course, they had a solid front door. That makes sense. Still, I continued to bang the hammer over and over and yelling to whoever could hear me in there.

"Tell me where they are! Tell me now!"

Nothing, absolutely no movement whatsoever.

"Why are you doing this to me? Come out here and show yourselves, you cowards!"

That's exactly what they were, cowards, and I was going to get the answers I wanted and the sleep I needed. Looking around for another way, the window just there to the right with the dimly lit lamp in the background. That was it. If they weren't going to come out here to me, I was going in there to find them myself.

Making my way to the window, a flash of color catches in the corner of my eye, and I can see the flashing lights pulling up closer. No, this can't be it. I have to get inside. I have to have answers, but before I can finish raising the hammer to swing at the window, I'm tackled and tossed into the grass.

"No, you can't! Make them tell me! Make them tell me where they are!"

Nothing I say matters. The torture those inside have been putting me through for days means nothing to anyone right now. I'm just some crazy person outside of someone else's house with a hammer screaming my head off. I get it. If it had been me, just some outsider looking on to this scene, I would be thinking the same thing. Instead, I laid there in the grass, completely spent. Every ounce of energy I ever had drained from my being, and I started to giggle. As much as the idea of jail scared the crap out of me, I was finally going to curl up on some bench or cot safely behind bars and find the sleep I've so desperately needed. In fact, I bet I'd be out cold before we rounded the block, and as they closed the door to the car, I looked back over at the front door I had just been beating on with a hammer and screamed at the scene in front of me. There stood a little old lady holding a cat that looked just like mine talking to the officer. It couldn't be. I had been watching that house for days. No one lived there, I just knew it, and as my disbelief as to what I had done washed over me, the static of the radio broke the silence as she looked over at me and smiled.

"We're still here."

www.ingramcontent.com/pod-product-compliance
Lightning Source LLC
Chambersburg PA
CBHW031545310726
48971CB00008B/2629